John Farman

The Very Bloody History of London

ARROW

1 3 5 7 9 10 8 6 4 2

First published in the United Kingdom 1999
by Arrow Books Limited
Random House, 20 Vauxhall Bridge Road, London SW1V 2SA

A division of Random House UK Ltd
London Melbourne Sydney Auckland
Johannesburg and agencies throughout the world

Printed and bound in Great Britain by The Guernsey Press Co. Ltd,
Guernsey, Channel Islands

RANDOM HOUSE UK Limited Reg. No. 954009

ISBN 0 09 940412 5

CONTENTS

To my late mum and dad
without whose help I'd never have been a Londoner
(or anything else come to that).

INTRODUCTION

When a man is tired of London, he is tired of life, for there is in London all that life can afford: Samuel Johnson

You might well ask me to explain why someone as humble as myself thinks he is qualified to write a history of probably the most historic and fascinating city in the world. No reason, apart from being a Londoner myself, owning a word-processor and having a publisher who thinks we might sell one or two copies.

Both my parents were proper Cockneys, born in London within the sound of Bow Bells and brought up in the East End (the poorer quarter). Following the mass exodus of women and kids from London during the war (in our case to Luton, for our sins), I returned to (and was brung up in) one of its more salubrious suburbs - Pinner to be precise. Well, that was until I saw the light and moved right into the middle at seventeen. Boy, did I hate the suburbs!

The Farmans, on my dad's side, I must confess, are a bit of a mystery. It's as if they didn't exist before my father's father (my granddad) and believe it or not I have no cousins - not one. When little, however, I do remember hushed talk of an uncle who ran away to be a vicar in Australia, and a great-uncle who shot a policeman, but we won't go into that now.

1

My dad, Lew, wasn't really fit enough to fight in the war so night after tedious night he had to watch from the roof of the Lloyd's Building in the City for fires resulting from the horrid Hun's incendiary bombs. Mum

stayed at home with my little - well - big brother Derek, who slept in a cupboard drawer during the blitz and has never really been the same since.★ (I suppose we really must let him out one day.)

On my mother's side (the Seeds), my other granddad - Joe Seed - was one of the very last London firemen to drive a horse-drawn fire-engine. He was famous for tearing through the cobbled streets of London with a little monkey (rather naffly named Joey) on his shoulder, in full fireman's outfit complete with miniature brass helmet (that's the monkey not my granddad) - there are even postcards to prove it. He met my grandmother, Amy, when the said amorous ape chased her down Ladbroke Grove, where she worked as a scullery maid. Joe eventually married Amy (obviously), but Joey, alas, was fired (sorry - bad joke). It has been suggested by my editor, rather unkindly I feel, that if my nan had married Joey instead of Joe, it could have been a very different story and that this book might have been a damn sight better written. I suggest, in defence, that indeed she might have found it easier to communicate with a monkey. Touché!

As for me, I've lived in and around London all my life and am rather proud to admit that, despite having been all over the world (well, Calais and the Isle of Wight), I've never been away for more than a couple of months and no longer have

★ *Only joking, Derek.*

2

any intention of doing so.

Anyway, I hope you, the reader, have as much fun reading my book as I, the writer, had writing it. I'm sure you'll realise that for every weird and wonderful story, every extraordinary character, and every fascinating place to visit that I've included, there are a million others waiting in the wings. Now, where do I begin?

IN THE BEGINNING

Maybe it's because I'm a Londoner that I love London Town:
Hubert Gregg 1947

Once upon a time in Olde England, three little streams trickled out of the Cotswold Hills and mingled at Lechlade. The resulting big, grown-up river, the longest in the country, meandered down through Oxfordshire, past Windsor, Chertsey, Richmond and then on and on for over two hundred miles through the densest forests, passing between Kent and Essex until it eventually poured into the sea at Gravesend. At this time, of course, none of these places except Kent was named and even the Thames (the river I'm talking about) wasn't called Tamesis until the late great Julius Caesar (coming soon) thought of it. The place the Thames passed through, which we now know as London, was in very early days a horrid, mosquito-infested swamp, populated by rather unpleasant beasts like mammoths, rhinos, hippos and elephants, evidence of which has been found at Heathrow airport. (Early jumbos?)

By the Way

According to the writer Geoffrey de Monmouth, London was founded in 1100 BC by Brut, the first King of Britain and great-grandson of Aeneas (tough guy god of Greek mythology). About a thousand years later a semi-mythical King Lud spruced it up a bit and called it Ludstown (as he would) and, quite honestly, if you believe all that you'll believe anything.

Much more likely was that it was a two-bit, run-down riverside settlement before being found and founded by the Romans on one of their all conquering away-days, halfway through the first century AD. It seems very probable that Celtic King Belin was responsible for a landing place on the south side of an earth wall surrounding a few damp huts. This watergate was later called Belinsgate (or Billingsgate).

STOP PRESS...

Just as I'd written this, I heard on the radio that, much to the surprise of all those know-all archaeologists, the remains of a prehistoric bridge have recently been found near the present Vauxhall Bridge. Carbon dating put it as far back as 750 BC. The learned boffins are still at a loss as to who might have built it.

Here Come the Romans

Imagine what it must have been like. It's 43 AD and there you are – Mr and Mrs Celtic-Briton and the kids, settling down after supper in your wattle and daub detached and thatched hovel in Lambeth (except it wasn't Lambeth then). Mrs Celtic-Briton, proud of her new pots and pans (thanks to Argos and the Iron Age) is industriously washing up

EARLY ROLE PLAYING

(nothing's changed there then) when you hear your early dog barking. Mr Celtic-Briton, muttering some ancient Celtic curse, goes to the front door to see what's up. He would have gone to the window, but it hasn't been invented. There, on the other side of the river, is a vast battalion of Italian soldiers in ridiculous, but none-the-less scary, outfits, their shields and spears glinting in the thin winter sunlight.

Mr Celtic-Britain always thought they'd be back. His great-granddad had told him hair-raising tales about the top Roman Emperor Caesar, pitching up almost a hundred years earlier, and how the fearsome English tribes, driving fearsome (if somewhat dated) two horse-power chariots, had shooed him and his army back to Rome where they'd come from.

By the Way

The Britons whom the Romans met still wore animal skins, still painted themselves blue (with woad), had long hair and, most peculiarly, shaved every bit of the rest of their bodies except for large moustaches (and that went for the men as well!).

Where to Put London?

This time the Romans were on a roll. For a start there were 27,000 of 'em and they were being led by Rome's very best general (Proconsul) under the orders of Claudius back home.

They'd wiped out anything that had got in their way and they were marching in a straight line (later to become Watling Street) from the coast at Richborough in Kent (where they'd landed) to find a suitable place to ford this vast river and eventually build the first bridge. They had to

x 27,000

get across so that they could get on with colonising the rest of Britain. As you've probably guessed (unless you're a bit dense) they stopped where London is now. This was largely because:

a) They were far enough from the sea for the surge of the tide not to have too dramatic an effect (like drowning them halfway across). You could still walk across the Thames as late as the twelfth century.

b) Both sides of the river (four metres lower then) were hard enough to bear the ends of a long bridge.

c) They needed a sheltered place inland, easily navigable from the sea, to bring supplies and troops right into the heart of southern Britain.

d) Gravel, on which London is primarily built, is known for being always saturated with fresh drinking water.

e) They were probably fed up with walking.

★ Worth a Visit? ★

All the most famous Roman roads converged on London and their mileage was calculated from a stone in the Forum of Agricola (called the London Stone). This can be found stuck in the wall of the Bank of China in Cannon Street.

By the Way

When geologists working for Meux's Brewery decided to break up years of concrete and brickdust to find what London was built on, they discovered sand – then gravel – then clay – then chalk – then greensand – then oolite (whatever that is) – then old red sandstone – and then, for some odd reason –

Devonian rocks. Presumably, beneath that they found a great underground lake of beer.

But London didn't become a town straightaway. The canny Romans first used it as a kind of transit place as, in those times, it was rather too boggy to do much building. Apparently, however, there was a naturally occurring firm path leading up through the marshes where St Paul's is now.

There are loads of different versions of how London got its name, but the most likely is that it came from the Celtic words Llyn (lake) and Dun (fort). London at the time was a huge marshy lake with little settlements perched on the gravel ridges.

Llyn-Dun   EARLY DUCK

By the Way

The drying up of the London gravel, caused by drainage and artesian wells, with the consequent disappearance of all the little streams that ran through it, caused the elimination of a weird disease known as the London Ague (a kind of malaria) from which many Londoners suffered. Cromwell and William III were just two of them. There was, however, another appearance in 1905 when the Piccadilly Line was being dug. Workers digging at West Kensington had to be treated for the smallest scratch that might have allowed contact with nasty water polluted over the centuries.

Whether or not our Celtic-Briton family survived is not certain (anyway I made them up), but we know the Romans used a lot of local labour to 'help' with the building of roads and the bridge which spanned the Thames at Southwark. The Romans soon turned Londinium into a hive of activity and it became a centre for commerce from far and wide. Being at the very edge of the war-torn Roman Empire it was able to concentrate on making money from selling cloth, hides, fur, gold, tin, lead, corn and, of course, double-decker buses.

★ Worth a Visit? ★

Probably the best museum in town is the Museum of London at City Wall. It has a wonderful section on early Roman London.

LOOK OUT! THERE'S A
BOUDICCA ABOUT

London seems to me like some hoary, ponderous underworld:
D.H. Lawrence

Only seventeen years later it all went horribly wrong. The Romans had been having a bit of trouble with the warlike Iceni and Trinovantes tribes who lived in a vast area around what's now called Norwich (not that they actually knew that then). A lady called Boudicca* (roughly translated as Victoria or 'Victory'), fiery ex-wife of recently ex-king Prasutagus, had stepped into the old man's shoes and become their leader. She'd become annoyed when, on her hubby's death, the cunning Romans claimed all her people's lands (not to mention the family fortune) instead of sharing it with her. When she put in a formal protest it rather miffed the all-conquering Romans, and they had the poor dear stripped and horsewhipped while her two daughters were raped for good measure. Now it was Boudicca's turn to be more than a little miffed and she decided to teach 'em a lesson.

KING SIZE
↓

The old girl must have been a terrifying spectacle, charging down what was their equivalent of the A11, her bottom-

* *Most people call her Boadicea, but it's WRONG. It was apparently a spelling mistake in a Renaissance manuscript.*

length, flame-coloured hair flowing in the wind as she steered her custom-built, self-drive chariot (blades on wheels etc.) at the head of 120,000 extremely annoyed Britons with jolly bad accents and worse haircuts.

★ WORTH A VISIT? ★

There's a fab statue of Boudicca in her chariot at the northern end of Westminster Bridge. It's surprising she and the chariot ever got there, for on close inspection there are no reins on the horses and practically no harness.

Boudicca first stormed the ancient Roman town of Colchester and when what was left of the 20,000 defenders realised the game was up, they rushed into the massive, half-finished temple of Claudius (who'd only just been promoted to being a god). Boudicca didn't have time to hang about; she simply piled brushwood round the outside and pot-roasted everyone – men, women and children; job done! She and her bloodythirsty blokes then hurried on towards Londinium, the Romans' new headquarters, destroying Chelmsford and St Albans and anything else that looked like a city on the way, and easily taking out a force of 5,000 Roman legionaries who came out to stop them.

By the Way

The heat from the massive fire in Colchester was so intense that the merchandise in a glass shop melted and formed weird-shaped puddles on the floor. I reckon I might have left a puddle on the floor if I'd seen that lot coming.

By the time Boudicca arrived in London, half the population, including most of the Romans, had fled out of the back door. She did rather well at first, massacring colonists and Brits alike (70,000 to be not very precise). At this time, most of the merchants in Londinium were foreign, from Gaul and Spain. Just to teach the Romans an extra lesson, she rounded up all the remaining noblewomen, who'd been living rather well up till then (but simply hadn't packed in time), and did horrid things to them - like hanging them up and cutting off their breasts and sewing them into their mouths so that they appeared to be eating them. (Disgusting or what?) She then stuck the women lengthwise on long, sharp skewers before leaving them out for all (who were left) to gawp at. What they did to the men is too gross for even me to describe (and, believe me, that's pretty gross!).

By the Way

Dig anywhere in the city down to a depth of four metres (better make it at night) and you will come across a thick layer

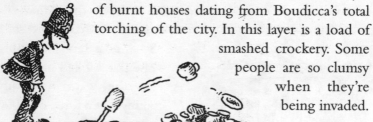

of burnt houses dating from Boudicca's total torching of the city. In this layer is a load of smashed crockery. Some people are so clumsy when they're being invaded.

Of course, poor old Boudicca then had to control her huge army of crazed warriors who'd been raping and pillaging anything left to be raped and pillaged. Unfortunately for her, they were rapidly forgetting how to fight properly. Gradually Suetonius Paulinus (Pauline for short?), the last great Roman general (Nero was in charge back home), having got over the shock of being trashed by a woman, began to get the upper hand in all the battles, despite being severely outnumbered (ten-to-one). The war-hardened and highly trained Roman soldiers were definitely not to be messed with if you wanted to stay in one piece.

The final battle was in 62 AD when the rough, tough Romans chased the Britons back to their parked carts where their families were waiting and massacred the lot of them, even the poor horses in the shafts (outrageous!). Boudicca, realising it was all over, put her hands up and admitted defeat. She then, rather sportingly (please debate), poisoned herself and her daughters (it really wasn't their year), so joining the 80,000 of her army who wouldn't be going home (and, presumably, saving Suetonius the trouble of killing her himself). Her body was never found.

★ WORTH A VISIT? ★

Take a pleasant walk down Gracechurch Street in the old City and, as you walk, consider that just under your feet were found loads of severed skulls, dating from around this time, which are thought to be all that remains of the Roman residents who got in Boudicca's way. There didn't, unfortunately, appear to be one with long red hair.

ROMAN TIMES IN LONDON TOWN: 100AD

To speak against London is no longer fashionable: E.M. Forster

Onward and Upward

After Boudicca's visit, London was just a pile of warm ashes, so it was time to start again. This time the industrious Romans put up huge and beautiful buildings like the magnificent Basilica and the 150-metres-long Forum (the largest building of its kind in the whole Roman Empire). The Forum became not only the city hall, exchange and lawcourts, but a huge market area to boot. The Basilica and Forum were roughly where Leadenhall Market is today. By the end of the first century the Governor's Palace was built, just below Cannon Street. Nearby at Thames Street was one of their amazing Roman bathhouses with underfloor heating and hot and cold running slaves to keep the fires going.

By the Way

In 1847, when the Coal Exchange was built, workmen found a freshwater spring which must have supplied the baths. It had later been converted by Mayor Sir Dick Whittington to supply water for the inhabitants and market people.

If you're wondering where the Romans did all their plays and games, worry not. Archaeologists recently discovered the remains of an amphitheatre near the Guildhall.

Sorry to disappoint you, but it looks as if they saved all the gory stuff like gladiator fighting for Rome, and they certainly didn't go in for giving their pet lions a good Christian breakfast.

The first permanent (albeit wooden) bridge was built in 90AD in much the same place as the present London Bridge. Before that they probably had a kind of wobbly construction running along the tops of boats.

By the Way

During the seven-year governorship of Julius Agricola from 80 AD, leading Britons decided they quite liked the 'Roman Way'. They were soon taking hot baths, drinking wine and even being seen in the odd toga.

Londinium, by this time, was becoming an important port, but the waterfront was a hundred metres north of its present position. The Romans built the very first Thames embankment out of massive oaks and, close behind, there were lots of wooden warehouses full of all those essential Roman imports, (garlic, pizza bases, Vespas etc.). By the second century the city was really booming and even warranted a visit by that great wall-maker and Emperor – Hadrian, for whom they rebuilt many of the major buildings, just to show off.

By the Way

A large bronze head of Hadrian was fished up from the bed of the Thames and is thought to have taken pride of place on the bridge (and on the rest of his bronze body).

By Another Way

Julius Caesar loved Southdown mutton and Whitstable oysters (from Whitstable), so these were exported from London back to Rome in great quantities, along with tons of corn.

Those Romans weren't daft, for, soon after the Boudicca incident, they'd realised that a horde-hindering city wall might be a good idea in case any more of those pesky native Brits got restless again. A huge, six-metres-high and three-metres-thick wall, of a million stone blocks was started in 190 AD, enclosing 330 acres. It was finished a hundred years later. Four huge entrances (and exits) to let people in (and out) were positioned at Aldgate, Bishopsgate, Newgate and Ludgate. The roads that led out from these gates were the first that the Britons had ever seen.

By the Way

One of the hundreds of barges used for bringing the Kentish ragstone from the quarries into the heart of Londinium was found under Blackfriars Bridge in 1962. It was seventeen metres long and under the mast was a Roman coin with the head of Emperor Domitian on one side and the goddess Fortuna, holding a rudder, on the udder (sorry!).

★ WORTH A VISIT? ★

Whilst you're at the London Museum (which I ordered you to go to), you can see the actual coin and the remains of the boat. Afterwards you can go into the gardens that surround the museum and touch the real live Roman wall.

The whole Roman province of England was split across the middle with London being made the capital of Britannia Superior, and York the capital of Britannia Inferior (no comment).

During the third century it appeared that all the ordinary folk moved out of central Londinium to what we'd now call the suburbs, leaving only the rich who were doing well. (Nothing's changed there then.) Most of the workshops and warehouses were moved away in favour of smart city houses for the rich merchants and government officials.

Smart Living

It is almost impossible to imagine, when you think of the heathens they replaced, but those early Romans certainly knew how to live. Fresh water was brought to their houses by lead pipes, and they had beautiful bathrooms – something the average smelly Brits only dreamed about. They even had hot air central heating for the cold winters, but this disappeared for maybe eight centuries after they'd gone.

A New Name

London was renamed Augusta for a short time to please the emperor-of-the-day in the fourth century (his title was Augustus). But then, in 410 AD, after less than 400 years of occupation, the Romans started withdrawing, much to the horror of the resident Britons who'd begun to rather enjoy the sophisticated Roman lifestyle and had grown a little soft when it came to self-defence. Their protectors were being recalled owing to the trouncing the Romans were getting back home in Rome from the barbarian hordes, and maybe also because here we had our own much closer hordes, whether Picts, Scots, Celts, Jutes, Angles or Saxons, practically hammering at the back door. Either way, poor little Britain was all alone in the world and no longer part of a great tough empire.

By the Way

According to Elton's (not John) *Origins of English History*, when the Romans finally scarpered, one could hear 'the groans of the Britons to Aetius, the Consul ...' claiming '... the savages drive us to the sea, and the sea casts us back to the savages; so arise two kinds of death, and we are either drowned or slaughtered'. Honestly, some people are never happy!

What Next?

Nobody is quite sure what happened to London in the next couple of hundred years. Was it occupied by Britons ruled over by the handful of Romans that missed the last boat back? Or was it taken over by the hordes of Germanic Saxons who were always coming and going? Or was it visited by aliens from the planet Zog? Or was it like a western ghost town - totally abandoned, with tumbleweed drifting through the streets? One can only hazard a guess.

We do know from a few old poems, however, that the Britons, who hated towns at the best of times, eventually shuffled in and were filled with awe, and even terror, at the huge Roman buildings that stood menacingly derelict. We also know that Vortigern, the new King of the Britons, invited over a group of Anglo-Saxons led by Hengist (the fierce leader of the Jutes) and Horsa to help keep out the Scottish Picts. By 604 (according to Bede's Chronicle), London was populated by heathens, just hanging around waiting to be kind of unheathened.

Historians now believe that London was never completely deserted, but that the Britons were so crap at anything vaguely practical (let alone technical) that the huge buildings, and the drains and roads, soon began to crumble through lack of maintenance. The only way we know that London Bridge held together is because we have records describing what fun they had chucking witches off it.

Silence Rules

Oddly enough, after the Romans went, the worst fears of the remaining Londoners were never realised. It was as if an historical blanket of silence descended over London. Trade practically ceased over night as the North Sea raiders plundered all the trade routes set up by the Romans. Alaric and his ghastly Goths had attacked Rome and were camping on her streets but, despite numerous attempts, barbarians never quite got through London's defences and after a while they all gave up, leaving London to enjoy a fairly peaceful time for nigh on forty years - practically a lifetime for our quick-to-die ancestors. London, it seems, didn't suffer as much as other places and had become largely self-sufficient. This might have had something to do with its being right on the outside of the empire and not in the thick of all the trouble.

Even so, the people left behind must have been like squatters in the once-beautiful city which began to disintegrate before their very eyes. Gradually, like a clockwork toy running down, this newly-independent London declined to the point where, instead of its being a mighty centre for trade, it became like an everyday market town, dealing in food, everyday household objects and the biggest cash crop of all time - fresh slaves.

HE DOESN'T LOOK THAT FRESH TO ME!

Londonburgh

Londinium re-emerged called Londonburgh, or London, in 601AD when the Pope declared that it was the place where his top archbishop, Augustine, should live. Augustine's main job had been to convert the heathen English to Christianity (and he got sainted into the bargain). Actually the Pope might have sent him to London, but Augustine ended up living in Canterbury. London finally got its own bishop in 604 and a nice wooden St Paul's Cathedral was put up by Ethelbert, the current king of Kent. His nephew Saeberht, king of the East Saxons, lived in the old Cripplegate fort (that's the bit of wall that you can touch at the Museum of London), and all the old Roman buildings were again used for various purposes.

London later began to flourish again, but the eighth and

ninth centuries remain a bit of a puzzle. It seems that during this period the major development was outside the city walls, north of where the Strand is now. This urban sprawl was called Lundenwic and was mostly used for farming and trading. Mind you, as soon as the Vikings started their bloodthirsty raids in the ninth century, anyone with any sense dived back within the walls for safety.

Golden Age

London was certainly changing. As it became more Christian, it was able to associate with Europe much more and eventually became a centre for foreign trade. King Alfred would look back on these years as being the Golden Age. So by 675 AD London was more or less a Christian city and was back on its feet, albeit still mostly through the slave trade. Best of all, it was becoming very rich, but worst of all, it was beginning to catch the eyes of those who wanted to get in on the action.

VIKING LONDON

London is a splendid place to live for those that can get out of it:
Lord Balfour 1944

The Viking invasion was divided into three main bits:
a) 787 – 855, when all they wanted to do was rape, pillage and make a general nuisance of themselves.
b) 902 – 954, when they tried to settle down here and be our mates.
c) 980 – 1016, when they had continual battles amongst themselves and with us Saxons, until Canute became the undisputed King of England.

Cash Only

Not a lot of people know this, but the Danish Vikings, as a general rule, far preferred hard cash to all the other spoils of war (molesting women, murdering and stealing whatever came to hand) and, as I suggested in the last chapter, news soon filtered through that London now had lots of it (hard cash, that is!).

WOULDN'T YOU PREFER THE WIFE?

In 839 the Danes stormed up the Thames in their scary dragon-headed longships and tried their first big takeover, only to be shown the door by the tough Londoners. A bit deflated, they went back and continued their raping and pillaging elsewhere until a few years later, when they had another go.

London Gets Trashed

Imagine the scene: 350 longships this time, chock-full of furry, ferocious, foreign foes leaping onto the embankments and over the city wall, slaying everyone in sight and then burning the city to the ground (not too difficult, it being nearly all wood and thatch). It was reported in The Anglo-Saxon Chronicle that 'there was great slaughter in London'.

The Vikings were not the brightest people in the world, however, for when they looked round and realised what they'd done, they decided a burned-out city is about as much use as a car with no wheels (even if they didn't know what a car was). Slightly puzzled, they went away to give the poor long-suffering Londoners a breather and time to build it all up again. They finally came back a year later in 872, but this time with their suitcases, wives and pets, ready to move in. They rather cheekily renamed the city Lundenevic.

GREAT DANE

By the Way

The Northmen, as they were called, rather liked Fulham and set up an encampment there. (In those days you could park.)

Alfred Saves the Day

After the Vikings had been in London a while, our King Alfred the Great of Wessex (reigned 871-99) managed to throw them out and let the Londoners, who'd spread into the suburbs, back in for protection. The Vikings had hardly had time to take off their tin hats and unpack their bags, before Alfred defeated Guthrum, their leader, in 886. He then 'persuaded' the Vikings to stay east of London (which they did for over 100 years) and restored the - er - restored and opulent city to the Kingdom of Mercia, before giving it to his son-in-law Ethelred the Unready who was sort of ready to run it (albeit very badly). It all came to a head in 892. Eight hundred ships full to the brim with Vikings (and their families) and horses (also with their families) turned up in the Thames Estuary and Romney Marsh having just been kicked out of Germany. But by that time, Londoners were even tougher and built dams to stop them getting any further. After being stranded for a few years they called it a day and decided to have a go at the Franks instead. And Alfred? The poor old chap only had three years of peace before he died.

By the Way

Ethelred had been nicknamed the Unready, not because he never was (ready), but because he was 'ill advised' and 'without council'.

Burned Again.

Oh dear, some people never learn the cardinal rule that if you build everything out of wood it's probably not the best idea to let little Erik play with fire. Some ancient Londoners did not learn, and their newly-built city was burned to a cinder again in 982. In fact, fire had become far more of a problem than the blasted Danes had ever been. In one way, however, it wasn't that serious, as at the time London was still surrounded by forests, and there were lots of freelance woodcutters and carpenters with nothing better to do than rebuild the city (who knows, they may've started the fire in the first place). The London craftsmen must have been pretty quick about the rebuilding because, by all accounts, there was plenty for the Danes to burn down the following year. It was just as if Alfred had never been there. At least he'd only ever burned cakes (allegedly).

By the Way

An ancient parchment dating back to the tenth century stated that the tolls set by King Ethelred, chargeable at Billingsgate for the use of a hithe (dock)★ were one half-penny for a trading vessel without sails and one penny with 'em.

Here they Come Again

Living in London must have been a bit of a nightmare - a recurring Viking nightmare. In 994 there came another huge combined Scandinavian attack from Norwegian Olaf Tryggvason and Svein Forkbeard, the exiled king of Denmark (and son of the daftly named Harald Blue-Tooth), who'd called in tons of Swedish Vikings from Russia to help them. They were held at bay, but in the end soppy Ethelred, who decided he'd rather pay 'em than fight 'em, had to dig deep and dish out pocketfuls of 'Danegeld' (16,000 pounds weight of silver to be precise) for them to get lost.

★*Hence Rotherhithe (castle dock).*

Then Ethelred did something even sillier. In a fit of pique, he ordered every Dane living in England – even the nice ones – to be slaughtered. The Danes were really miffed this time and made Ethelred pay £36,000 to keep away. Olaf stuck to the deal, but Svein (whose sister was one of those murdered) was still understandably cross and, realising also that it was a brilliant way to get rich quick (and being a two-faced lying ba – barbarian), kept coming back, each time demanding more. Not only that, but he'd got it into his head to be King of England as well as Denmark (which, by the way, he'd just got back) and, having conquered most of the larger towns, realised that he'd better take London as well.

MORE PLEASE.

Ethelred the Unready saw that he was onto a loser, and, when he was finally ready, hightailed it off to Normandy, leaving the hitherto loyal Londoners to fend for themselves.

'Sod that!' they cried – as one – and simply held up their hands and begged for mercy. Later, Ethelred sent a saucy French postcard promising to try harder if they'd have him back.

★ WORTH A VISIT? ★

Should you find yourself in Kingston (almost London), look for a weathered lump of stone outside the Guildhall. Almost unbelievably, it is the stone that seven Saxon kings were crowned upon – from Edward the Elder in 900 to Ethelred the Unready in 997. Set into the stone are coins dating from each of their reigns.

Cnute (or Canute, or Knut)

In 1014, when the Danish King Svein Forkbeard died, his successor Cnute (pronounced Ker-newt), who just happened to be his son, decided he wasn't prepared to fight any more and went home thinking it OK to leave a strong Danish garrison in London. His timing was a bit dodgy, because

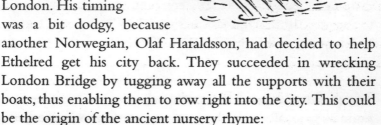

another Norwegian, Olaf Haraldsson, had decided to help Ethelred get his city back. They succeeded in wrecking London Bridge by tugging away all the supports with their boats, thus enabling them to row right into the city. This could be the origin of the ancient nursery rhyme:

London Bridge is broken down,
Gold is won, and bright renown.
Shields resounding,
Warhorns sounding,
Hildur (who?) shouting in the din!
Arrows singing (what?),
Mail-coats ringing - (how?)
Odin* makes our Olaf win!

So. . .

Briefly, Ethelred died and Cnute came back to claim England. Most of England gave in, but Ethelred's son Edmond Ironside, holed up in London, decided to put up a fight. When he died,

* *The Vikings' top god*

however, his dad's widow Emma, obviously hedging her bets, went and, rather perversely, married Cnute who promptly became King of all England. Embarrassing or what! It's now fifty years to go before the Battle of Hastings and London still only has a population of 12,000, a fraction of what it was in Roman times. Having said that, it is by far the biggest port in the country, sending to, and receiving ships from Paris, Antwerp, Ghent, Bremen and Hamburg. The ships bring with them many foreign merchants who are happy to settle here.

By the Way

Although Cnute didn't exactly conquer us, England was made to pay one eighth of the nation's wealth, £72,000, as a tribute, and London paid a further £10,500. Nice deal if you can get it.

King Cnute of All England

London gradually came back to peace and prosperity under its new king. It was divided into wards which ran themselves, trying their own crimes and generally minding their own business(es). Londoners, by this time, were fed up with fighting, putting out fires and building up knocked-down walls, and for the first time felt free to speak their own minds without fear of repercussions. However, London's men were rather miffed at having to wash more than once a month, and comb their hair, in order to get off with the nice-looking Danish babes.

SKRUB AS DIN SKIDERIK

I THINK THAT MEANS SHE LIKES ME

By the Way

There used to be a little river that went from the Elephant and Castle to the Thames called the Tigris. It is said to have been dug by Cnute as a passage through the marshes from Rotherhithe to Chelsea so that his fleet could avoid London Bridge when he laid seige to London.

During Cnute's nineteen year rule, London became rich and powerful once more. Cnute was once described as 'one of the conscious creators of London's greatness'. The city finally surpassed Winchester as England's capital city and has not looked back since. Cnute was not only King of England but of Denmark as well, which made him top man in the whole of Northern Europe and, best of all, he chose London as home.

By the Way

All that business about Cnute being told by his creepy courtiers that he could hold back the sea was slightly wrong. It actually happened on the Thames at Lambeth, which was tidal. Perhaps they were trying to time it so that the high tide was just on the turn, making it look as if it was his orders that sent the water back. Just a thought. Anyway, these days we've got the Thames Barrier (see page 250).

★ WORTH A VISIT? ★

Clapham is one of the oldest areas of London. In the earliest times a Saxon noble called Aelfrid gave his wife, Werburgha, thirty hides of land in the manor of Clappeham. A Danish nobleman called Osgood Clapha lived there, and at the riotous party given to celebrate the marriage of his daughter in 1042, the star guest, none other than your actual King of England, HardaCnute (Cnute's son), got so sloshed that he fell over and promptly died.

Much later, Clapham started to become populated in a big way by terrified Londoners fleeing the plague and, later, the Great Fire. Recently Clapham suffered an even worse pest - yuppies - led by Thatcher the Great (Queen of Inflated Property Prices), who forced out the natives and turned practically every shop selling things you might actually need into a wine bar.

FANCY YOU LIVING HERE
AS WELL, RUPERT

All good things come to an end and so, with Cnute and his successor Hardacnute dead, Emma and Ethelred's lad Edward became King in 1042. As Edward's mum had been brought up in Normandy, he brought all his Norman mates into London to take all the best jobs. Talk about paving the way for a Norman invasion. Eventually he moved away from the walled city to his brand new Palace of Westminster which broke with tradition. Kings had always stayed 'within walls'.

While Edward was busy moving, his brother-in-law, head anti-Norman, Harold, Earl of Wessex, was gaining support. In 1066, when Edward was a-dying-o, he gave Harold the nod and Harold became King.

By the Way

Edward founded Westminster Abbey in 1065 and ten days after it was finished, he was able to be buried in it. Some kings have all the luck.

★ WORTH A VISIT? ★

You can still visit Edward's tomb at Westminster Abbey. Well, the base anyway. A magnificent, jewel-encrusted, golden structure was built by Henry III when he rebuilt the Abbey in the thirteenth century. But later, when Henry needed cash, he plundered Edward's fabulous shrine and now only the base remains. Nearby lie the remains of Henry and his son Edward. Edward, rather touchingly, had all his flesh boiled off so that it would be easier to take out his bones and carry him before the army when fighting Scotland. Grim job, but someone had to do it.

JUST WILLIAM

London: a dirty little pool of life: B.M. Malabari

Everyone knows about William the Conqueror and the Battle of Hastings (if you don't, rush out and buy the very fabulous *Very Bloody History of Britain* by . . . er . . . me). But what did they find when they arrived at the capital city?

Walls mostly, and a lot of angry faces looking over them. Those early Londoners proved to be a bit of a difficulty. They had become rather good at defending the city, and William's forces, though having had a fairly easy conquer so far, weren't that many in number.

When William and his troops pitched up, therefore, he found London Bridge closed. He and his hommes then carried on up the river, having set Southwark on fire. No big deal; everybody set fire to Southwark when they first arrived (it was almost a tradition). They finally waded across at Wallingford, way up stream near Oxford, and trudged back down the other side towards London, destroying as they went along all the farms (and farmers) that provided London with its grub. But William's reputation had gone ahead of him, and the Londoners were feeling just a little nervous behind their high walls. Silly really, they were plenty strong enough to keep him out. But most of the earls and barons had already disappeared back to their distant estates to see what their wives had been up to (at knight), and so many of

IS IT REALLY A WHOLE YEAR, MY LORD?

their best soldiers had been chopped down at Hastings, that they felt more than vulnerable.

A posse, therefore, led by the Bishop of London, rode out of the city to meet William (who had already got to Berkhamsted), with a view to offering him the crown anyway. Instead of the Norman nasty they were expecting, the Conqueror turned out to be rather a nice chap, and terribly reasonable. He told them that, as far as he was concerned, they could carry on as usual; he had no plans to make their lives hell and even offered them the rather chummy and now famous King William's charter. Here's a bit from it:

William the King greets William the Bishop and Gosfrith the Portreeve and all the Burgesses in London, French and English, friendly. And I will give you know that I will that ye be worthy of all those laws that ye were in Edward's day. And I will that every child be his father's heir after his father's day. And I will not suffer that any man offer you wrong. God keep you.

The group from London promptly invited him and his men back for a very special tea and the Normans entered the city to great pomp and circumstance, with the aldermen giving William his own set of keys to the city, which was rather kind I think (especially if he ever wanted to come home late).

By the Way

When William was crowned King of England, a little later, there was such a joyful uproar that William's knights, who were waiting outside, thought that some huge treachery had taken place and promptly torched the whole of Westminster. Whoops!

Just William's

Almost as soon as William had eased his aching and extremely large backside off his no doubt aching and extremely large horse, and had managed a look around, he realised he'd better set about building bigger city walls to protect the city from the east and west. London, as you now know, had been untouched by the invasion, but many of the little towns and hamlets surrounding it were in real bad shape.

FOR SALE
ONE FAT
CAREFUL
OWNER

It must be said at this stage that although, unlike the Saxons, the Normans were rather good at towns, William was hardly ever at home in the city. Being a conqueror for a living involved a lot of nights fighting away, whether against the English, the Scots, the Welsh or the French, or anyone else of a foreign inclination.

By the Way

It's interesting to note that in the Domesday Book (the huge volume that William had drawn up to list everything he owned, right down to the last serf, so that he could tax 'em rotten), London and its contents were not mentioned. It was almost as if he didn't want to push his luck. Little farming villages that are now regarded as part of central London, like Fuleham (Fulham), were omitted although Stebenhede (Stepney) and Chenesitun (Kensington)★ were put in.

★ *I bet you couldn't find as much as an allotment in Kensington these days.*

★ WORTH A VISIT? ★

If you fancy taking a look at the real live Domesday Book, get thee down to the Public Records Office in Chancery Lane.

Tower Time

Although for years after the Conquest your ordinary Londoner remained in his little wooden thatched hut, King William wanted a fab castle to protect himself, his large household, his royal guard and all those treasures he nicked on his travels, not only from foreign invasion, but from the actual Londoners themselves. He built the first Tower of London out of wood but – as the three little pigs later realised – wood isn't a lot of good where fires are concerned, so he decided to build a new one out of the same stone that had been used for the city walls. The White Tower (called such because they painted it white) was twenty-eight metres high, with walls five metres thick and three turrets. It was finished by 1100.

William had called in architect Gundulf, who was probably a bit of a misery as he was nicknamed 'the weeping monk of Bec'. I bet that being called away halfway through rebuilding his own cathedral at Rochester (he was the bishop there, you know) didn't cheer him up, nor the massive gale of 1090 that blew all the Tower's supporting scaffolding down, flattening 600 houses (not to mention their inhabitants). Actually, Gundulf couldn't have been that bad a builder when you consider that the White Tower was never taken by storm and is still standing 899 years later - now known as the Tower of London.

★ WORTH A VISIT? ★

One of London's most prestigious relics is the Chapel of St John in the White Tower. It's seventeen metres by nine metres. Unfortunately, all its crosses, images, plate and gold were melted down by grumpy old Edward VI who hated anything remotely flashy.

By the Way

You can now also visit the dungeons under the keep at the Tower. There you can view a dear little cell called 'The Little Ease', only 1.2 metres square - too small for the prisoner to sit, lie or stand comfortably, let alone entertain his friends.

YOU'LL FIND IT DELIGHTFULLY COMPACT

WELCOME

One of William's mates, Ralph Baynard, built himself Baynard's Castle, a massive Norman fortress, just inside the western wall. Baynard's Castle was finally destroyed in the Great Fire of 1666, but one tower was left standing until 1720.

Archaeologists found bits of it when they were poking about in 1972.

Westminster Hall

Westminster soon became the preferred home of the Norman noblemen and between 1097 and 1099, William's boy, Rufus (William II to you), built the magnificent and still standing Westminster Hall, which he called, rather smugly, a 'mere bedchamber' compared to the palace he had in mind. Fair enough, Rufus, but I reckon I could live with a seventy-two metres long and twelve metres high bedroom (crikey, I could get my house into it more times than I like to think about).

The Hall became the centre of justice and administration for all of England, which is interesting because it was almost two miles outside the city walls. Westminster became very much the King's domain and, for centuries after, there has always been a bit of edginess between the Crown and the City.

Norman Laws

Unfortunately the Normans were a little strict when it came to laws for the poor inhabitants. Here are a few examples:

• All Londoners were told what to pay their servants.
• They were responsible for their neighbours' behaviour and would be punished for *their* wrongdoing.
• They couldn't buy anything from the markets until the King and all his henchmen had been round and bought the best stuff first.
• They were forbidden from going outside the city walls to buy anything.
• They were told when they could and couldn't go out on the streets.
• They were locked into the city at night (curfew time). Lepers were kept out.

• They were ordered to extinguish all fires and lights at said curfew time. The massive bell of the Collegiate Church of St Martin's tolled to let everyone know and all the parish churches followed.

• They were periodically told what they should or shouldn't eat or drink.

• They were even made to keep their rather common dogs indoors while the Normans' more 'genteel' dogs were allowed to roam the streets.

HE ACTS LIKE HE, OWNS THE PLACE

By the Way

If a 'bonded' man managed to slip into London (or any walled city), and was able to stay undetected for a year and a day, he was allowed to stay as a free man.

LONDON AFTER WILLIAM

If I could choose the place where I die it would be London, because
then the transition from life to death would be hardly noticeable:
Hammersmith graffito 1979

Parishes and Wards

Early London was divided into hundreds of little parishes and
wards and nobody seems to know when they started or why
the parishes, of which there were four times as many, didn't
match their boundaries with the wards'. Come to that,
nobody seems to have much clue why there were so many
churches in the first place – over a hundred within the city
walls. Perhaps it was just that there were so many more people
to go to them, or that the area all around London was so
boggy that, if they had built them there, they'd eventually have
disappeared into the gloop – without a song or a prayer!

★ WORTH A VISIT? ★

Kilburn, which is now regarded as almost Central London (and
a province of Ireland), began as a little suburb of Westminster.
In fact it was just a priory with three nuns and a chaplain. If you
don't believe me, go along to St Mary's Church, Priory Road
and there, if you're keen, you'll find a little piece of fifteenth-
century brass, only six centimetres long, with a nun's head on it
– all that remains of the medieval priory.

MI?

The main road north out of London ran from London Bridge to where the Roman Basilica had been, and then up to, and through Bishopsgate where it left the city and made its way quietly into the countryside (see Gracechurch St and Bishopsgate now). There were a couple of east-west roads: the main one called Thames Street (which it still is) ran between the city wall and the Thames. By this time the river banks had been strengthened and built upon. It was to the honeycomb of warehouses, in the little alleys running from Thames Street to the river, that all the merchandise and foodstuffs from abroad, eventually found their way. The warehouses were a hive of spice merchants, ships' chandlers, coal merchants, wine-importers, wool and silk dealers, and more.

All the fish, as today, were taken straight into Billingsgate in the actual fishing boats that caught 'em. The merchandise was sold to the public from areas like Cheapside, Eastcheap and Westcheap ('cheap' is old English for 'barter') which were just collections of stalls and booths lining the streets and alleyways.

As for making things, all the streets were named after the products they specialised in. Wood Street, Milk Street, Ironmonger Lane, Mobile Phone Alley etc. Giltspur Street was where all the knights came to buy new armour and weapons (you never think of that, do you?) and where they could get stuff repaired. One of the smelliest parts of town, apart from Billingsgate, was at the end of Newgate Street and called the Shambles to which the doomed animals, bought at Smoothfield (now Smithfield), were led to their bitter end.

How It All Worked

The City of London was run on two levels. On the one hand it was ruled by the current king, and on the other it was self-governing with a mayor (from 1200). The Mayor was a sort of go-between for the king and the city elders, but also acted as the king's deputy – a tricky position, as you must realise.

The Norman kings had always been strong, but soon worked out that life would be a hell of a lot better if they managed to keep the city aldermen (heads of the wards) on their side. Henry I, realising this, allowed London to collect its own taxes and choose its sheriffs but he took a little something (like a huge bung of cash) for granting them the privilege.

Guild Money

Not only that, but Henry creamed off a nice little income from the ever-growing London guilds (collections of craftsmen linked for self-protection) in return for confirming their rights and making sure no other non-guild members muscled in on their action.

By the Way

Henry I's charter to the Londoners did, however, allow them to farm Middlesex for £300 a year (a snip) and hunt throughout Kent and Surrey.

The city overlords, combined with the guilds, eventually wielded such power that they could start telling certain royalty what to do, especially if said royalty were making a balls-up of things or, as was mostly the case, were hardly ever in the country. Although they were away, however, these Royals soon learned how important it was to keep London sweet.

All the Fun of the Fair

St Bartholomew's Fair, at Smithfield, was founded in 1133 by Henry I's court jester, Rahere, who decided to abandon his jokey ways and form a Priory and Hospice (St Bartholomew's Hospital is still there). To finance it, he organised a huge cloth-fair for three days every August from which the Priory took tolls from all the stallholders. Alongside this the Corporation of London held a cattle fair. Over the centuries the fairs turned into a sort of medieval theme-park with tournaments, fire-eaters, jugglers, dwarfs, regular executions and various other super family attractions. Later Bartholomew Fair became a centre for serious productions of plays. By the 1600s, however, it was nicknamed 'Ruffian's Hall', a place for duels, fights, and lashings of gross indecency and debauchery (sounds rather a laugh) and was finally closed down in 1855. It was then 'respectablised' in 1868 when Smithfield Market was established. Today it employs 1,500 people and sells 15,000 tons of dead animals a year (which is still pretty disgusting if you're a veggie).

The Clink

Way back in 860 the notorious Bishop of Winchester, known as St Swithin to his mates, erected a Colledg of Preestes in which he ordered that there must be one 'small dank cell' for keeping monks or friars caught doing naughty things. By the twelfth century, King Henry I (William II's successor) was very matey with the Clergy, and so in 1107 the latest Bishop of Winchester thought it quite cool to have a place near the King's court in Southwark. He built a relatively modest mansion and a chapel, but his successor Henri de Blois had bigger ideas and built the seriously stupendous Bishop of Winchester's House in 1144 which housed hundreds of his retinue (servants etc.).

In the courtyard he built a little prison, later known as 'the Clink', for those chaps that fell foul of the law, and another for women – the first women's prison ever. The following bishop, Theobald (also Archbishop of Canterbury), was a real character, for besides his no doubt arduous clerical duties, he ran twenty-two brothels along Bankside (the Lord moves in mysterious ways). He drew up a code of rules for 'women living off their bodies' and, if these rules were broken, he would 'accommodate them in his cells' and charge them for the privilege. At this early stage of the Clink's history, however, the female prisoners did not face the threat of torture. The only things they had to worry about were starving or feezing to death. But you wait.

By the Way

The whole area around the Bishop of Winchester's palace became famous for the more 'basic' attractions in life and, even as far back as the twelfth century, visitors were warned against 'crowds of pimps – actors, jesters, smooth-skinned lads, Moors, flatterers, pretty boys, effeminates, paederasts [look it up], singing- and dancing-girls, belly dancers, quacks, sorceresses, extortioners, magicians, night-wanderers, mimes, beggars and buffoons'. (Sounds brilliant – like Soho on a Friday night!)

Crusaders Return

When the first crusaders returned to Britain they were full of lurid stories of the fantastic new tortures they'd witnessed out East. Those heathens certainly knew all the ways of making one talk. The Clink, by the way, was one of the first prisons to try a few of them out. They started with a 'furca' or 'oubliette' (from the French 'to forget') - a deep hole under the cellars of the Great Hall where prisoners were simply dropped in and promptly forgotten about: a 'theu' - a special women-only type of stocks, and a 'cucking stool' - even nastier than a ducking stool, which again was just for the ladies. The New Great Hall, built by Henry of Yeovel, was much grander and housed the men's prison in the vaults.

ER-EXCUSE ME

★ WORTH A VISIT? ★

Amazingly, you can still find the last remaining part of the hall in Clink Street SE1 (next to the Clink Museum). All that's left is the beautiful, four metres in diameter, rose window, standing where it was discovered in 1814.

It was now that things in the Clink started to hot up a bit. The women's section was given tiny ventilation gratings, at street level, so that they could beg for food from passers-by. Often, if no one fed them from outside, they would starve to death. The poor dears would arrive stripped to the waist, their heads shaven, having been pelted and whipped by the jeering crowds. Some were held fast in the bloodstained pillories or whipping posts while rocks, rotten food and dung were thrown at them (and all that for a parking-offence). In the dungeons was a fabulous array of shackles and manacles specifically designed to be as uncomfortable as possible, and the screams of tortured men and women could be heard throughout the night. Heigh-ho!

Madness

Often, the appalling treatment would drive men and women completely barking mad. There were no doctors nor medical treatment (not so much as an Elastoplast or aspirin) and the gaolers were so badly paid that they would extract by force what money the prisoners had. If an involuntary inmate wanted bedding or candles, for instance, he would have to pay for it. Any money given by charity would be snitched before it could benefit the prisoners. Prisoners even had to buy their own food, often at extortionate rates,

WILL YOU BE TAKING BREAKFAST, SIR?

from the gaolers, and it was, most times, rotten. Women prisoners often had to sell their clothes for food and drink, and would end up naked in the freezing, dark and lavatory-free cells (sometimes their mess would remain for months on end). The gaolers, for a cut of the action, would even allow favoured Madams (brothel keepers) to operate from the cells.

Torture

But that was nothing. Some unlucky prisoners were beaten and chained up in such a way that not only made sleep impossible but caused paralysis. Or they would be made to stand naked in the flooded cells (at high tide) until their feet rotted. As if that wasn't enough, they could undergo authorised torture on the rack or be crushed to death under heavy weights, which was no fun whatsoever. That could be the origin of the expression - getting something off your chest. From 1229 heretics would be imprisoned for the rest of their short lives in tiny, totally dark dungeons.

★ WORTH A VISIT? ★

The little prison museum in Clink Street is a bit of a rip-off, but you do get quite an idea of what it must have been like.

By the Way

Newgate Prison was built in 1218 and was to remain for 560 years as a debtors' prison.

Matilda or Stephen?

In 1135 there was a good example of how important it was for the Royals to keep London sweet. Henry I ('the king who never smiled') died from a meal of bad eels, and nobody was quite sure who should succeed him. Some thought it should be Matilda, his stroppy daughter, and some thought it should be his nephew Stephen (Stephen certainly did). A civil war followed.

London didn't get on with Matilda, who was quite simply a bossy cow. She'd been engaged at the age of seven to the Holy Roman Emperor (bad start) and it had gone to her head. On top of that, she'd been brung up in Germany and we all know what Germans can be like.

When she took the city by force in 1141, she treated the top brass in London, who'd already made Stephen the King, like imbeciles. She had Stephen imprisoned in Winchester, whipped his crown off him and headed on up to Westminster to put it on herself in the Abbey. But London would have none of it and let all Stephen's supporters through the gates. The terrified Matilda and Co. dashed out of the back gate and

YOU WON'T BE NEEDING THAT ANY MORE-MY LORD

hightailed it to Oxford. She never ever got back in, and had to sit on the sidelines to watch her son Henry II be made King when Stephen died.

As you can imagine, Henry was only too aware of what they'd done to his mum and was determined to crack the whip and get control. He started by taking away all the privileges that his granddad had given them and made them empty their pockets taxwise as never before.

Jews Get it Bad

Don't go thinking that the Germans were the only ones to persecute Jewish people. We English have done our fair share over the ages, particularly in London. During the twelfth century, the city was filling up with many different foreign communities. Most of them, because of their various specialist trades, were accepted, admired and even welcomed - but not the Jews. Having brilliant business brains, they tended to go in for financing and moneylending, but although they turned a good profit from Londoners they were despised by all and sundry. Consequently they were allowed no legal rights and, because of this, successive monarchs were able to squeeze money out of them willy-nilly.

Not Invited

When Henry II died in 1189 and was succeeded by his son Richard I, Jews were barred from the coronation knees-up (because they weren't Christian). But many of them brought gifts anyway (which was rather decent of them, in the circs). When they arrived, however, the loyal, Godfearing (well - Christian God-fearing) Londoners turned on them - killing thirty and then looting many of their homes (that's Christianity for you). Much later, in 1256, the poor Jews were accused, falsely, of crucifying a Christian child at Lincoln and 102 of them were brought to Westminster. Eighteen were hanged and the rest went to prison for a long, long time. As if things weren't bad enough, when Italian bankers came over to try to cash in on the action, setting up shop in Lombard Street, Edward I forbade the Jews to lend money on pain of death. He then accused them of coin clipping★ and put 300 to death while seizing their possessions.

In 1290 things got even worse. Every single Jew was suddenly arrested and banged up in prison and then ransomed for twenty grand (which Edward I used to build a couple of castles with). Eventually, in 1306, all 3,000 of them were kicked out of the country and the Crown grabbed their houses. (Not very friendly!)

★ *Cutting bits off coins and melting them down to make new ones.*

Frequent Fires

William Fitzstephen, a monk, writing in 1174, described London as full of immoderate drinking (nothing's changed there) and frequent fires. The two seem to go together somehow. He was not wrong (there were four major burn-ups between 1077 and 1136), so in 1189, during Richard the Lionheart's reign, they finally passed a law forbidding thatching and stating that at least the ground floor of every building should be built of stone. Mind you, I dare say it didn't worry our Dick, as he spent all his time in France or crusading in the East.

By the Way

London Bridge was by this time in a rotten state and hardly usable. Every time they tried to rebuild it, some idiot would accidentally set it alight again. In 1209 a stone bridge was completed which was to last in various forms until 1830. 'Cor blimey' (see *Quaint Old Cockney Speak*), if it had lasted nine years longer, it could have had its photo taken. Early engravings show that from around 1200 there were rows of tall houses and touristy type shops on either side of the bridge, but these were removed in 1752.

During the great fire of 1212, the buildings at both ends of London Bridge caught fire and, as usually happens when both ends of a bridge give way, all the sightseers and firemen caught in the middle leapt into the swirling river. 3,000 poor souls were reported to have drowned in the scramble to get on to the rescue boats.

Fitzstephen also described what is now Middlesex, just north of London thus:

There are pasture lands and a pleasant space of flat meadows, intersected by running waters, which turn revolving mill wheels with a merry din [speak for yourself]. Hard by there stretches a great forest with wooded glades and lairs of wild beasts, deer both red and fallow, wild boars and bulls. The cornfields are not of barren gravel, but rich Asian plains such as make glad the crops and fill the barns of their farmers with sheaves of Ceres stalk.

The vast forest he describes is what would now be rich suburbs of Golders Green, Hampstead or Highgate, and the pleasant meadows are, like as not, naff golf courses these days.

By the Way

Glass was only affordable to the very rich, so most houses had no proper windows to speak of.

By the Way

Richard I was so strapped for cash due to the enormous cost of the Crusades that he said that he'd sell London willingly, if he could find a buyer. Where was Richard Branson when he needed him?

Sport for All

Just as now, London was a great place to be young in, provided you weren't poor (nothing's changed there then). Every Sunday afternoon, crowds lined the river to watch a sort of water-jousting: young men stood at the pointy end of boats, holding lances and aiming them at fixed targets in the middle of the river (don't ask me why). The city folk would also enjoy theatrical performances, at Clerkenwell (Clerk's Well) and at Skinners' Well (now long gone), like the portrayal of the torture and suffering of martyrs (I love a good comedy). Most popular of all were the horridly cruel and bloody 'sports' of bear- and bull-baiting, which were regarded as wholesome fun for all the family, and cock-fighting which was, almost unbelievably, encouraged in the schoolroom. Children could often be seen trundling along to school with the poor cluckers clutched under their jackets.

In the warm summer evenings young men would be seen to engage in all sorts of early sports from long-leaping to javelin chucking, from wrestling to stone throwing, while maidens danced merrily in the moonlight (as maidens do).

When the Thames froze over, as it did every year, it would be time for ice-skating or should I say 'ice-skiing'? Young lads would bind the shinbones of animals (dead) to the bottoms of their feet and carry two long poles to project themselves along at breakneck speed.

Feeling Poorly

The level of medical knowledge in the twelfth century was appalling. The Jews and the clergy were the first to practise in England but when the poor Jews were driven out of the country things went from bad to worse. John of Salisbury (a mate of Thomas à Becket) thought the whole medical profession useless. He reckoned they had two golden rules: 'Never mind the poor; never refuse money from the rich'. (Does that sound familiar?)

Bad John

On Richard's death in 1199, his brother John became King and a very unpopular one at that. He lost whatever cred he had with the powerful London merchants by demanding even higher taxes to fight his nice new war with Normandy. Eventually even John's barons had had enough and forced him to sign away a lot of his massive power in the Magna Carta of 1215. In this it was also stated that London could elect its own mayor (or rather the barons could elect one).

Don't go thinking that the Magna Carta was a massive leap towards democracy, however. It was more like a way for the barons to control things themselves, especially as they were now able to pull the strings of the puppet mayor whose job was to look after the interests of business. The people, by the way, who were badly paid and worse housed, could jolly well look after themselves.

Eating Out

I don't know about you, but I always think of restaurants as fairly new inventions, but in Norman London there were lots of public eating-houses and cookhouses, like the one by the river near Smithfield. It was open every day and would serve up all kinds of roast beasts and a wide variety of fish. The food was sort of segregated, with coarser, cheaper food for the poor and more delicate fare for the rich. It's interesting to note that practically no one ate their greens in those days. Believe it or not, these houses were the first to run a comprehensive takeaway service for the odd knackered post-Norman who couldn't be bothered to cook at home on a particular night.

By the Way

In 1212, at Fitz-Ailwyne's Second Assize, it was ordered that the hundreds of cookshops along the Thames be stripped down and cleaned up so that they could no longer have lodgers (at one penny a night). This law was later relaxed, but they still ordered that these places be only run by freemen and, on no account, by foreigners. Some people think that the term 'Cockney' comes from the men who owned the cookshops.

A City at Last

London was now looking like we imagine a proper city to look like. The streets buzzed with the cries of pedlars and market traders and, at night, with the giggles and entreaties of ladies of loose virtue. There were taverns and alehouses, bakers and tailors, and horses and cattle everywhere. Each little immigrant community lived in a particular area as it still often does.

In 1256 the City obtained authority to build a channel to bring the water from the Tyburn river at Paddington back to the City. Towards the end of the century, conduits were set up to distribute this water but they soon fell into disrepair, creating a rare breed, the water-carrier, who peddled filthy Thames water door-to-door, in equally filthy leather panniers.

By the Way

The first elephant to be seen in England since prehistoric days, arrived in London in 1256 and seemed constantly depressed as it joined the

FOR GOD'S SAKE – CHEER UP!

first polar bear in Henry III's menagerie. The bear drew huge crowds as it hunted for fish in the Thames.

By the Way

In 1261 the export of wool and the import of cloth were banned. Woad was the only dye permitted for use on wool, so foreign woad merchants weren't allowed to settle in the city and had to sell their merchandise on the quay, as it was landed. The English woad trade was later ruined by the introduction of indigo.

★ WORTH A VISIT? ★

If you're walking down King Edward Street in EC1, pop into the Post Office Shop. It is on the site of the old Greyfriars Monastery which was built in 1225 by nine Franciscan monks. The last remaining buildings were finally destroyed in 1897, thanks to the extension of the General Post Office.

By the Way

Covent Garden became a market for fruit and veg around 1264 selling the surplus produce from Westminster Abbey gardens.

PLAGUES AND THINGS

The vilest alleys of London do not present a more dreadful record of sin than does the smiling and beautiful countryside:
Sir Arthur Conan Doyle 1930

Up to the thirteenth century, the government had been wherever the king (or queen) happened to be at the time. This had meant carting around a whole mega-gaggle of civil servants and their secretaries. Apart from anything else – no faxes, E-mails, and no proper storage for the mountains of parchment scrolls that were beginning to pile up – there were the problems of feeding this entourage and all the sanitary arrangements caused by such. It became obvious that there should be a centre for all this mounting administration and, in medieval

England, London became the obvious choice.

Henry III (1216-1272) not only saw the need for this but also began to realise that life would be a darn sight more comfortable if he stayed in one place for longer at a time. But as he still had to travel, he made sure his various castles throughout the kingdom were kept up to scratch for him and the (now greatly reduced) gang of hangers-on – should they turn up.

Three Departments

There were three main departments that had to be set up to keep things in some sort of order:

a) the Exchequer (so called because of the checkered tablecloth on which they counted the cash) which dealt with collecting all the funds necessary to run the country.

b) the Chancery which oversaw all the law and justice throughout the land, having dealt with the mess that the clergy had made of it.

c) the Wardrobe, an odd name for the department that dealt with the monarch's personal expenses (not the crowns and robes and stuff).

But Henry III was becoming less and less popular with his subjects and, realising he was in a bit of a dodgy situation, decided to transport his French missis, Eleanor, away from London up the river in the royal barge. Unfortunately the London mobs hated her even more than him (because of her outrageous extravagance), and the royal couple was forced to turn back because of all the stuff that rained down on them as they tried to go under London Bridge. Can you imagine if we did that sort of thing these days?

It was the city merchants who hated Henry more than anyone else, and they were mighty rich and powerful. 'Nauseatingly rich' the potless Henry called them. The final showdown came in 1263 when Simon de Montford, representing the City, led a rebellion and defeated the King. However, after Simon was rather badly killed at the battle of Evesham two years later, Henry punished the City big-time for having turned against him and supported Simon. He fined them £17,000.

By the Way

OCH! JUST WHAT I'VE ALWAYS WANTED

Simon's head was sent as a kind of thank-you present to the Earl of March's wife who'd helped to trash de Montford's new plan for government.

Edward's Turn

When the highly unpopular Henry III died in 1272, the country had to hang around for a couple of years to meet their new King, Edward I, because he was still away doing his thing in the Holy Land. To say they were deliriously happy to see him was no exaggeration. The streets of London were hung with the finest silks and tapestries, the conduits that normally carried water flowed with both red and white wine, and the aldermen and city bosses threw handfuls of gold and silver over the royal procession. Can't see us doing that these days. All our lot get are little plastic flags (if they're lucky).

Famous Londoners No.1: *Richard de Podlicote*

The very earliest attempt to steal the crown jewels was in 1303 when Edward I was away fighting William Wallace in Scotland. Richard de Podlicote (Keeper of the Palace of Westminster) broke into the crypt of the Chapter House in Westminster Abbey and, with the help of four monk mates, escaped with a cool seventy-five grands worth of prime sparklers. Podlicote nearly got away with it, but was caught with the loot still on him. Edward I was understandably rather cross when he got home, and had poor Richard flayed alive. His skin was nailed to the door of the Chapel of Pyx where bits of it are still to be seen to this day (let that be a warning, if you're visiting the Tower).

By the Way

The execution of William Wallace, the Scottish rebel, was the big story in 1305. At the mock trial in Westminster, he was given no chance to answer the charges. As executions go, it could have been better. First he was hanged, then disembowelled while still alive (guaranteed to make ones eyes water). When dead his four limbs were sent to four distant locations and his head was stuck on a spike at London Bridge for all to see.

This began a horrid custom. Heads of condemned men were lightly boiled in the gatehouse by its keeper to preserve them, then dipped in tar to preserve them even longer, before going on display. By 1598 there were up to thirty heads at any one time displayed on the bridge. Ah well, I suppose it was company for them.

Rich Have it Good

Conditions in London were improving rapidly, but only if you were loaded. For instance, the rich could have their own bath with the first piped (wooden) water from the River Tyburn, and nobody complained if the windows steamed up, for windows were a new fangled luxury. The rich certainly lived well, as we can see from all the paintings that they left. Also, Italian fleets were beginning to arrive regularly in London introducing silks, fruits, rare spices and Greek wines. Before that, the only access to exotic goods had been due to the returning Crusaders.

I TOLD YOU I'D BRING YOU SOMETHING EXOTIC, MY DEAR!

Londoners Go Hungry

But if you were poor it was a different story. There had been two major famines in London: one in 1086 and another in 1150. But in the early years of the fourteenth century a series of wet summers caused the harvests to collapse. 'There followed this famine, a grievious mortality of people, so that the quick might scarcely bury the dead.' All the cattle then died from malnutrition (no grass) and the starving Londoners turned to other sources for their meat. They started with horses then progressed to dogs, and then it was even claimed that they began to eat their own children for lunch and kidnapped others to eat later. Children that were unfortunate enough to be thrown into prison often had a worse fate awaiting them as the starving inmates fell upon them and started eating them while they were still alive. It never rains but it pours.

Another Edward

In 1326 Edward II made another attempt to curb the independence of the City by force. It all went terribly pearshaped and ended with a frenzied mob chasing him through the streets. When they failed to catch him they pulled down the Bishop of Exeter (Edward's treasurer) hacking his head off with a bread knife.

However, Edward was not to escape from a painful demise. He was the king that met his end with a red hot poker rammed up his bottom at Berkeley Castle.

The Londoners were in a fighting mood and riots were a regular part of medieval London life. The guilds, failing to find anyone better to have a go at, turned to fighting amongst themselves. It was really weird - suddenly pitched battles broke out among all the various guilds. In one street, the tailors started fighting the goldsmiths and before they could take breath, all the others joined in. Later, Italian traders were picked on, accused of sleeping with English women (a dastardly crime) and of siding with the French in the Hundred Years' War.

Pollution

The explosion of manufacturing had many by-products, the worst of which was pollution. Unlike today, there were no controls on what you did with all the crap-waste products you didn't want. The breweries and tanneries along the River Fleet, for instance, chucked in all their horrid muck and so did all the people who lived along its tightly packed banks. London was fast becoming a seething rats' nest of stinking passageways, their overhanging gables so close that the streets below were in continual twilight.

By the Way

A baker called Richard drowned in a cesspit of human excrement when the floorboards gave way under him while he was at work.

The powers that be tried to create huge dumps outside the city walls but, people being people, and Londoners being obstinate, they seldom bothered to use them – and by now it was 80,000 people not bothering to use them. Why should they, when they had a perfectly good river close by to throw everything in? Eventually the filth built to such a pitch that something just had to snap, and it doesn't take a degree in bacteriology to work out what that was.

By the Way

In an effort to clean up London's streets and ward off the inevitable, melters of tallow and lard were turned out of their premises, all the dung was removed from the Walbrook watercourse, and four men were elected to kill any swine found wandering on the King's highway.

By Another Way

Good news: the first public lavs were opened in London in the 1350s. Bad news: they were directly over the poor old River Fleet. They became so successful that their combined output eventually put paid to the actual flow. Don't get too excited, however – lavatory paper didn't exist and they had to resort to the old Roman sponge on a stick and a pot of salt water routine. These lavatories were occasionally cleaned by 'rakers' or 'gongfarmers'* who were paid extremely well (and I should think so too).

* *Gong was the ancient word for lav and contents of such!*

But all it needed was a catalyst, and that came in 1348 in the form of a bunch of holidaymaking rats who scurried off their tour ships carrying their own individual travelling fleas who, in turn, all happened to be carrying a nice little disease called 'the bubonic plague' or 'Black Death' or 'Great Mortality'. Britain hadn't been the first port of call, for the disease had swept the globe from China to India to Italy to France, scoring a death toll of many millions. It arrived first in Dorset and quickly marched on London, infecting everything in its path.

Into the Pit

A year later, EVERY DAY over 200 ex-Londoners were being dropped into the special pits dug at Smithfield. And can you believe this, only two years later than that, half the population of London was, as they say in Cockney rhyming slang, 'brown bread'? Just imagine that, half of all your mates and half of all your rellies six feet under. Many churchmen thought it was God's way and the beginning of the end of the world, and who can blame them? One of the big headaches was where to put the mountains of stiffs that were beginning to litter the streets as the good folk of London obeyed the order to 'Put out your dead'.

★ WORTH A VISIT?

★

In 1349 Sir Walter Manny, the Mayor of London, purchased thirteen acres at what is now Charterhouse Square because all the city cemeteries were full to bursting. If you ever go to the square, just think, you will be walking over 50,000 plague victims. It's worth a visit anyway for its beautiful Georgian houses built in the 1700s.

The poor devils in those days had no clue as to what caused the disease. Was it the air? Was it the earth? There were lots of daft superstitions. Was it the appearance of a raven, a heron alighting on a church, or of an ox that had somehow rung one of the many alarm bells? They even slaughtered all the cats and dogs in case it was their fault, and painted pretty red crosses on the bolted (from the outside) doors of 'plague houses' (residents within) to try to contain the infection.

By the Way
Scientists didn't discover the nature of the plague bacillus until the beginning of THIS century.

The truth was that the disgusting condition of medieval London, with its open lavs and sewers, filthy drinking water, its lice and flea-ridden houses, and inhabitants who wouldn't have known a bar of soap if it had been thrown at them, certainly didn't discourage the legions of rats that scurried in and out of the people's houses and over their very beds (and heads).

Leprosy
It was no time to be a leper in these days. Lepers were driven from anywhere that people congregated and made to carry bells to warn of their approach. They had no rights, especially

to any family inheritance. It seems a bit ironic that lepers were often given rotten food to eat, when it was probably bad food that caused the disease in the first place.

In 1310, Richard le Barber, the first Master of the Barbers' Guild, was appointed with all his fellow barbers to keep watch on the London gates, to prevent lepers getting in. Later, Edward III ruled that all inner-London lepers should be thrown out of the city gates which led two 'leper-spitals' to be opened - one in Southwark (the Loke) and the other in Kingsland (Hackney).

Smallpox

John of Gaddeston, a famous physician, wrote a book in 1305 called *Rosa Angelica* in which he claimed that the only cure for smallpox was to wrap the patient in a red blanket and make sure that everything he touched was red until he was entirely cured (success guaranteed). To treat gallstones he recommended that a paste of ground dung, headless crickets and squashed beetles be rubbed on the stomach. That's my kind of doctor!

Pirate Alert

In 1370 the Lord Mayor was told that several pirate ships, with hundreds of armed men, were lurking in the mouth of the Thames and he ordered a watch of forty men at arms and sixty archers to keep lookout from the Tower. On Tuesday it was the turn of the drapers and tailors, on Wednesday the mercers and apothecaries, on Thursday the fishmongers and butchers, and so on throughout the week.

A few years later, John Philipot, a rich merchant, fitted out a fleet of ships at his own expense to catch the ringleader of the ever-increasing bands of pirates that infested the Thames and local waters. He was made Mayor by his fellow citizens.

Population

I think it's about time to give you some idea of the population in London at the time. In 1377 there were 44, 770 men and women aged over fourteen (there are nearly 7,000,000 now), while in the rest of the country the major cities of the time were relatively tiny. York had 7,248, Bristol 6,345, and Coventry 4,817.

Enough's Enough – the Peasant's Revolt

The peasants in the rest of the country weren't daft either; they realised that, with a huge percentage of the work-force forcibly sent to heaven due to the plague, they had much more clout when it came to stating their claims to the beastly bosses. This all came to a head with the Peasants' Revolt in 1381, the clearest and heaviest class war that Britain has ever seen before or since. What sparked it off? There were lots of reasons, but the main two are that:

1) The greedy landlords were trying to breathe life into the dying feudal system, to solve all their labour problems, but the peasants were fed up with serfing.

2) The Government tried to impose a poll tax (much like Margaret Thatcher in the 1980s) on a country that was nearly out of food and extremely fed up already.

Individual parishes tried on obvious scams such as lying about the number of inhabitants, just so's the poll tax charge to the individual would be lower. When these porkies were uncovered the authorities went crazy and came down so horribly hard that the peasants of Essex, Kent, Norfolk,

Suffolk and Cambridgeshire decided enough was enough and marched on London, smashing and burning manor houses on the way. The Kentish rebels were led by a couple of chaps called Wat Tyler (an ex-soldier) and John Ball (a vagrant ex-priest) and met with the others on 12th June.

Where's Richard?

They waited for ages to meet the well-nervous fourteen-year-old King Richard II who came up the Thames by barge to Greenwich from his hidey-hole in the Tower of London. Unfortunately, the crowd was so huge and so cross when he got there, that he was forced to turn back. Wat Tyler was on a roll, however, and he and his men ran to the nearby Marshalsea Prison and let all the prisoners out, torching the Marshal's houses into the bargain. Then they went on to Lambeth and burnt all the Chancery records. A quick trot over London Bridge and they were in Fleet Street, where they set fire to buildings and ransacked the Fleet Prison. Then it was up the road to the New Temple, murdering anyone who got in their way, where they destroyed all the lawyers' records (tee hee), before beheading anyone who even looked like a lawyer. It was mayhem.

By this time the Londoners, who'd been well fed up with the government anyway, joined in and trashed John of Gaunt's hyper-luxurious Savoy Palace. All the clothes, furnishings, gold and jewels were burnt and thrown into the Thames. 'What a waste,' I hear you cry.

Tyler had said there was to be no looting and he beheaded anyone who did, along with any lawyers, clerics or people he didn't like the look of, including any individual who looked remotely foreign (a touch extreme, methinks).

By the Way

While Tyler's men were ransacking John of Gaunt's palace, about thirty of them found his cellars and commenced one of the greatest drinking sessions ever recorded. When the signal came that the whole place was to be sealed up they were so pissed they didn't hear a thing. Their cries were heard for over a week, but nobody went to their rescue. Maybe that's how the term 'dead drunk' came about.

The following day, brave little Richard II, who'd had to watch all the horrendous goings-on from his window in the Tower, finally met the thousands of rebels at Mile End and agreed that the whole idea of feudal services should be abolished, and that the peasants could rent land for 4d an acre (just under 2p) per year. He also assured them that the rebels would be free from any repercussions for all the death and destruction that they'd caused, but that any real traitors on either side would be parted from their heads. This seemed to pacify the rebels who, truth be told, never had much against the king in the first place.

Wat - an End

But Wat Tyler hung around when the others started to slope off. He hadn't broken into William the Conqueror's impregnable Tower, prised out the Archbishop of Canterbury, chopped off his head (it took eight blows) and stuck it (mitre and all) on London Bridge, for nothing. The following day King Richard went personally to Smithfield to try to work

out what Wat was really after. Apparently, Mr Tyler was so insolent to the King that the Mayor, William Walworth, pulled him off his horse and stabbed him to death. Young Richard, realising the - er - delicacy of the situation, pacified the mob by standing up in the saddle (he *was* on a horse at the time) and offering to be the rebels' leader (see *Quick Thinking in Ancient Times*) and led the mob off towards Clerkenwell to quieten them down.

By the Way

During their rampage, Wat Tyler's unruly mob set fire to Winchester House above the Clink (see page 46), pulled down the Bankside whorehouses and beat up the women. One of the brothels was owned by Mr Walworth, the mayor - the guy that did for their leader. Small world!

★ WORTH A VISIT? ★

Jack Straw's Castle, the famous pub on Hampstead Heath, was named after one of the leaders of the revolt who sheltered in the original coaching inn (a mere hovel) while on the run - until caught and executed by the king's men. Charles Dickens often used to walk across the Heath to have lunch there.

By the end of June all the risings had been put down and most of their leaders 'subdued'. But the poll tax was no more and, for centuries to come, kings and queens of England were never allowed to forget the spectacle of peasants rampaging through the streets of London.

Money Problems

In 1392 Richard II was a little short of the old readies and wanted to borrow a grand off the Londoners. They not only refused but killed an Italian merchant who said he would lend it. Richard went mad and chucked the Mayor, sheriffs and many other prominent men in prison. In the end, the Londoners said they were sorry, showered him and his missis with presents and offered the King £10,000. I wonder if my bank manager would go for that scam.

By the Way

It was officially recorded that Richard II died of over-eating, but later reports suggest he was poisoned with toadstools sprinkled on his food.

Crime Watch

London, at this time, had its fair share of crime, but must not be thought of as much worse or better than anywhere else. For a start there wasn't a lot of stealing as, apart from the very rich, no one had anything worth stealing. Those caught for serious crimes didn't hang around in prisons long, as they were whipped, mutilated, pilloried or branded and sent home (if they had one) or they were simply executed. Way back in 1283 in the City, an act demanded that each of the wards should provide six strong householders as watchmen at night. This didn't really improve until the nineteenth century.

The Oldest Profession

Most of the prostitution was in and around Southwark★ (under the control of the Bishop of Winchester) as was a lot of the crime, until it gradually spread up to the Strand and

★ *For centuries known as 'the blind eye', a refuge of all low-life.*

69

into Covent Garden. Prostitutes weren't allowed in the City, but elsewhere the women were tolerated although, during various times in history, they were required to wear little badges (suggestions on a postcard?). An act in 1352 went further,

stating that 'common, lewd women' weren't allowed to dress like their proper, respectable sisters. I never thought they did!

Topless

During Richard II's reign it became law that 'pretty women' (prostitutes) should only be allowed in certain parts of town. Any loose woman found out of her area was forced to remove the top half of her clothing so that everyone would know what she was. Chilly but effective.

Other Punishments

• Imprisonment or pillory (with a stone hanging round the neck) for saying nasty things about the Mayor or anyone else in high office.

- Pillory for cheats, users of dodgy dice, false check-boards, forgers of title deeds, beggars pretending to be dumb, blind or anything else etc.
- The seller of duff wine was made to drink it.
- The seller of disgusting or putrid food was made to eat it.
- Women of bad reputation were only allowed to wear certain clothes (no wool, fur or silk).

Debt

In the fourteenth century, fear of going to prison for debt hung over most citizens (I know the feeling!), and there were lots of private debtors' prisons all over London, only too willing to take you - for a fee. Usually the only way that you could get out was for your family or friends to raise the cash you owed. If they didn't, it was hard luck. A debtor generally had to rely on charity simply to stay alive.

Some prisons were different, however, being regarded as very much part of society. If you were in the Fleet prison, for instance, you could do work in or out, for it meant that you could bring your gaolers money to bribe them with. Some prisoners could even go out for the evening if they could find the right amount of cash. The whole business was a farce.

GOOD NIGHT, SIR.
DON'T BE HOME
TOO LATE!

Say After Me

A great stunt a felon could pull was to call on 'benefit of the clergy'. Way back in 1351 priests and churchmen were one of the few groups that had any sway with the King (he was a religious nut). Edward III had been persuaded, therefore, to legalise an old custom. If any convicted person could read this passage from Psalm 51 which went, 'Deliver me from blood guilt so shall my tongue sing thy righteousness', implying that they were not only educated but of a religious nature, they would be put under the jurisdiction of the much more lenient ecclesiastical courts. This was far preferable to risking one of the King's prisons like Marshalsea, Newgate or the dreaded Clink. It doesn't take the Brain of Britain to realise that those who couldn't read, could simply be taught to say the line parrot-fashion by the local priest (for a price – naturally).

Famous Londoners No. 2: *Elizabeth Moring*

In 1398 Elizabeth Moring, who ran an innocent-looking embroidery business as a front, was banished from the City for inciting her lady employees to sleep with friars, chaplains 'and all other such men'.

★ WORTH A VISIT? ★

If you want to see a real, genuine medieval church, untouched by fires or civil wars, look for the alley next to No.8 Hatton Gardens. This leads into the private road of fab Georgian houses called Ely Place. Halfway along you'll come across the beautiful St Ethelreda's. St Ethelreda was quite a girl by all accounts, having this nasty habit of marrying men and then refusing to go any further (if you know what I mean). Her second husband, Prince Egfryth, would have none of it and, cutting his losses, forced her in 679 to enter a nunnery where she suffered a massive tumour on her neck and died. Her sister

NOT ANOTHER HEADACHE?

called Sexburga (Egfryth might have done better with her!) opened her tomb sixteen years later to find her skin totally unblemished. That's saints for you.

THE 1400s

Oh, London is a fine town,
A very famous city,
Where all the streets are paved with gold,
And all the maidens pretty.
George Colman 1797
(Especially on the Kings Road on a Saturday afternoon:
John Farman 1999)

Super-Dick and the Guilds

By 1423 there were more than a hundred guilds in London, covering every trade from leather workers, clock-makers and fishmongers to second-hand cart dealers, and they were becoming ever so wealthy. Several of the massive edifices they built themselves, like the Saddlers' and the Skinners' Halls, are still on the same site centuries later, as are some of the schools they set up later for their children (Merchant Taylors, Haberdashers etc.). If you didn't belong to a guild it was difficult to do business, as guild membership was the only way of becoming a citizen and you couldn't trade if you weren't one.

The subject of guilds is a bit boring, so I'll move on, but I will just add that, unlike the modern trade unions that still fight for the workers' rights against the bosses (if the government allows them to), it appears that the guilds were far more democratic, protecting anyone – bosses and workers alike – and were far, far more powerful.

Famous Londoners No. 3: *Dick Whittington*

I always thought that Dick Whittington, with his cat, hat, pavements paved with gold etc. was just a pantomime character (oh no you didn't), but I now realise I was wrong. Come to think

A RIGHT DICK!

LONDON

of it, I also always thought of him as a cross-dresser, as I've only ever seen him in pantos, played by long-legged starlets with big feathery hats and no trousers.

By the Way

Dick's 'cat' was pure fiction, but proper historians say the term referred to a boat much used at the time. How d'you walk to London with a boat?

Richard Whittington was a real person who was born wealthy (his dad was a Sir) and came to London as an apprentice. He became Lord Mayor four times between 1397 and 1420 and went on to become the wealthiest merchant in town and famous for giving tons of it away.

By the Way

Just to indicate how rich a Dick he was; when Henry V (hero of Agincourt) brought his highly desirable French bride home, Dick gave them a sumptuous and scrumptious banquet at his own expense. Mind you, that was nothing. When the new Queen remarked on the cost and the fragrance of the special fire (made of precious woods and with expensive spices chucked on), joker Dick promptly threw on £60,000's worth of bills (nearly £24,000,000 in today's money) representing the cash that the King owed him.*

* *Whittington had been the banker to both Henry IV and V.*

Mr Whittington rebuilt the hitherto disgusting Newgate Prison, provided pipes for London's fresh water, and paid for the beautiful floor and windows, as well as for half the library, of the magnificent Guild Hall (just in time, as printed books were just around the corner).

★ WORTH A VISIT? ★ *(Ring up)*

The staggeringly beautiful crypt, built of Purbeck marble, is still there today and is the most extensive medieval crypt in London.

By the Way

Some mayors (they were mostly recruited from the guilds) used their office to improve Londoners' morals. Sir William Hampton, a fishmonger, punished strumpets and caused stocks to be built in every ward to teach vagabonds a lesson (don't be poor!). A later mayor replaced stocks with cages. (That's progress for you).

In 1422 Henry VI came to the thrones of both England and France when only tiny (nine months old to be precise). This severely limited his early decision-making abilities (speech would have helped). As he got older, it became obvious that he had inherited his grandad's loopiness (from the French side – *naturellement*), but luckily he married a dame called Margaret who was most certainly sane. It was a perfect marriage. He stayed in London while she was away practically all the time, fighting

the Wars of the Roses against the Yorkies, who were after her old man's crown. Extremely decent of her, don't you think?

Henry was a weedy, wimpy fellow, by all accounts, and suffered from melancholia all his life. Even before the war started, he could usually be found skulking round the cold and gloomy Westminster Abbey, creeping about the clergy and searching for the ideal spot to be buried in. He was passionate about, and founded lots of, posh schools including King's College Cambridge and Eton.

By the Way

Henry became obsessed by women's parts (in his late teens) but not how you might think. He would run screaming from the room if one of the 'larger' ladies-in-waiting entered wearing a low cut gown.

By Another Way

Henry would wander the streets of Windsor (where Eton is), getting off on warning little boys about the disgusting things that went on in his court at the Castle.

Talking of boys, in 1406 a proclamation was issued forbidding the sports of Foteballe, Hokkying, and Cockthreshing in the streets of London. 'Foteballe' was obviously football, while 'hokkying' appears to have been a curious game where young men and women on 'Hokkedayes' lassoed strangers and demanded money for charity. 'Cockthreshing' was either cock fighting or simply cock throwing which was rather popular.

Famous Londoners No. 4: *Jack Cade*

It seems a trifle difficult to imagine, but in those days, with no police force and an army usually away at wars, it didn't take more than a large crowd of rowdy rebels to take over London. This happened in 1450 when a rabble led by a certain Jack Cade pitched up at Southwark and persuaded their mates on the other side of London Bridge (mostly London traders hacked off with the government) to lower it and let 'em in (just like gatecrashing a party). They were demanding a series of reforms, and the heads (removed) of certain members of the government. For nearly a week, brave Jack strutted about the City gaily proclaiming himself the Lord of the City, and even managed to – er – 'shorten' a few important people, but he always crossed back over the bridge to Southwark at bedtime.

★ WORTH A VISIT? ★

Jack Cade used a pub called the White Hart, as his headquarters in Southwark, which was only demolished in 1889. If you want to see an identical pub from roughly the same period (and very close by) visit the amazing George Inn on Borough High Street. Mine's a pint!

On the seventh morning poor old Jack found the drawbridge up and, as he didn't fancy getting wet, he decided to go home. Unfortunately he was severely wounded and died in the cart taking him off to prison.

Welcome to the Yorkies

The Yorkists were getting the better of the war with Henry's (or Margaret's) Lancastrians and in 1461 decided on a victorious away-day to London. The crowds went crazy when they arrived (they'd never thought much of weedy Henry) and made Edward, a big (six foot four inches), strapping, handsome, jolly sort, their King (Edward IV). It's a real swizz – you can't do that sort of thing these days. Henry was kept in the Bloody Tower and Margaret scooted off to France where she probably opened a bar.*

Here Comes Edward

Edward turned out to be even more popular with the city leaders and merchants than with the hoi polloi because, being a wheeler dealer in his own right, he didn't need nearly so much tax money as all those short-of-funds ex-monarchs, in order to live in the manner to which he was accustomed.

He did muck up big-time later, however, when it was decided that he should marry the King of France's little sister for diplomatic reasons. He surprisingly, and to the shock of all concerned, announced that he'd met this gorgeous widow and mother of two, called Elizabeth Woodville, on the triumphant journey to London, and worse, instead of taking her for a mistress as they usually did, he'd married her in secret. This pissed off his nearest and dearest so much that he was forced to flee the country, probably passing the warlike Margaret, who was now on the way back. Is this confusing?

The end result was that poor old Henry, who'd been languishing in the Tower all this time, got his big shiny hat back and was King again.

* *She probably didn't: Editor*

By the Way

The highly virtuous Liz Woodville refused Edward's sexual advances even with a knife at her throat, insisting on 'no nookie before marriage'.

WHERE'S THE RING?

Not For Long

However, the restoration of Henry didn't last, as Edward teamed up with the Duke of Burgundy and hopped back over to trash poor Margaret once more. Henry simply went back to his old room in the Tower for another six years before Edward (probably) had him murdered in 1471- just to be on the safe side.

It must sound as if life in England was pretty precarious with all these wars and changeovers at the top. In actual fact, wars in those days seldom affected the common man (unless he was killed) and London seemed to carry on perfectly well, whoever seemed to be King-of-the-Week.

★ WORTH A VISIT? ★

The present church of St Botolph in Aldgate was built in 1744, and is well worth a visit. But the history of the St Botolph's that was there in 1471 is even more interesting. When Thomas the Bastard, of Falconbridge, who'd gathered a force of ships in support of poor little Henry VI (he doesn't sound that much of a bastard!), landed near the Tower, he was met by fantastic fortifications. He sailed back to Aldgate and there broke through the defences. The citizens, tricky to the last, then dropped the portcullis capturing all the soldiers who'd burst in. They then wrenched it up again and attacked the rest with such vigor that they were able to chase Thomas the Bastard's men all the way to St Botolph's where hundreds were cornered and slain.

The Bloody Tower

It was during this next bit of history that the Tower became known as the 'Bloody Tower'. It had always been home to the best and most famous prisoners but many of them, in the early days, had gotten out alive. From 1471 onward it really wasn't the place in which to make plans for your future. Over a relatively short period, Henry VI, Edward IV's brother George the Duke of Clarence, and, oh yes, the two little princes, along with everyone who looked as if he could cause even the slightest irritation to the King, were never to see the light of day again.

By the Way

What a way to go! The Duke of Clarence ended his life upside down in a barrel of malmsey wine.

Where Are We?

A brief resumé. Edward is King again, Margaret's back in France, poor old Henry's dead, and except for the odd rebel attack, London can start to look forward to a period of peace and tranquillity. For twelve years, until the now grossly corpulent Edward IV's death in 1483, London, through massive expansion in trade with those of a foreign disposition, continues to become stronger and stronger compared to other English cities.

Hanseatic League

There was, and had been for some time (since Henry III), an area right in the heart of London called the 'Steelyard' which had been the stronghold of the Hanseatic League – alien merchants from a group of German ports, who'd banded together as protection from pirates. It was a throbbing nightmare of tightly-packed lodgings, warehouses and counting-houses populated by German traders. Henry had, for some bizarre reason, allowed them to operate as a separate little state, abiding completely under their own laws. For my money this is one of the things that makes London great.

The Hanseatic League kept themselves separate from the rest of the population, drinking their own wine, exchanging their own currency, and refusing any women or games (or games with women) within their walls. Although the Steelyard was known to bring business to the city, Londoners hated the cocky Germans, so when Edward IV said they couldn't play any more – revoking all their rights – it made him jolly popular.

By the Way

There was an old saying that went: 'The Hanseatic merchant buys a fox-skin from an Englishman for a penny so that he can sell him the tail for a florin' (much more).

The Germans were always one step ahead and cut the English out of any of their dealings. Edward then tried to close the Steelyard completely, but those canny Krauts made sure that there was a massive foreign embargo on our woollen cloth, which brought our merchants to their knees.

By the Way

The Germans weren't the only foreigners to get the cold shoulder from Londoners. An Italian visitor once complained that 'Londoners have such fierce tempers and wicked dispositions that they not only despise the way in which Italians live, but actually pursue them with uncontrolled hatred. They look askance at us by day, and at night they drive us off with kicks and blows of the truncheon' (and that was before the European Cup).

Edward eventually gave in and let the Germans have all their rights back and even a lease on the Steelyard. The League carried on for a couple of hundred years and the actual complex was only built over in 1852 to make room for Cannon Street Station.

Famous Londoners No. 5: *William Caxton*

You probably won't remember when telly first hit your average sitting-room, but it must have been a bit like when William Caxton brought over a printing machine from Germany, in his excess baggage, and first started printing and importing books in 1476. London was bang at the centre of the new book world when Caxton opened his first printing shop at 'the Red Pale' in Westminster, with his assistant - the ridiculously (if not inappropriately) named, Wynkyn de Worde.

It's fair to say that for years and years London had a complete monopoly on the printed book, and a hundred years later there were twenty-four printers in town.

As well as the craving for religious books and all things spiritual, there was also a growing market for trash and the more low-brow stuff (as there still is) with folk tales, broadsheets, fables, fairy stories and almanacs, available for all.

By the Way

Wynkyn de Worde was real smart business-wise and moved the whole operation to Fleet Street, which then became associated with printing until the mid-1980s when most of the big newspapers moved to the Docklands.

By Another Way

As soon as the great King Edward IV was dead, he was left to lie stark naked, for all to see, for over twelve hours before being moved to St. Stephen's Chapel, Westminster, where he hung around for another eight days.

Here Comes the Law

By 1500 there were a record-breaking 2,000 students learning law. To be honest not nearly that many stayed the seven-year course. Being mostly the sons of rich merchants they used it as an excuse to come to London and party for a couple of years, maybe picking up a few tips that might help them with future disputes over property.

TUDOR LONDON

*The chief advantage of London is that man is always
near his burrow:* Hugo Meynell (1720-1808)

During the sixteenth century, London's population went
through the roof but not, as you might imagine, because
everyone was having a marvellous time in the bed department.
The city, for years, had been right bang in the middle of the
ever-flourishing and highly profitable wool trade, and farmers
and landowners had realised that by filling their fields with
dozens of dozy baa-lambs, they could make much more loot
than by the arduous and chancy business of growing crops.
Sheep were brill. Not only did they look after themselves
(munching grass and growing wool without even thinking
about it) but, the minute they caused any trouble, they could be
eaten. To cut a short story shorter, thousands of farm labourers
who'd been ploughing and
sowing and harvesting for a
living, were put out of work and
gradually began funnelling into
London, having no
doubt heard Dick
Whittington's old
'streets paved with
gold' yarn.

YOU JUST WATCH IT!

Too Many

London now had too many people for its size. To give you
some idea; in 1509 the population was about 50,000, by 1583
it had leapt to 90,000 and by 1603 it was 200,000 – a rise of
300% in a century.

Instead of spreading outwards and then upwards, as most sensible cities have a habit of doing, London went upwards and then outwards, causing the upper storeys above the teeming, seething streets to hang over the lower ones to such a degree that neighbours, living opposite each other, could practically shake hands (or anything else for that matter). Soon it became almost impossible for the light to penetrate the already too-narrow streets, making them dark and dangerous and a happy hunting ground for thieves, pickpockets and, no doubt, life assurance salesmen.

GUESS WHAT THEY'RE 'AVIN FOR SUPPER

★ WORTH A VISIT? ★

If you feel like visiting a real live Tudor palace and, behind it, almost deserted ancient gardens that will instantly throw you back to Henry VII's time, go thee forth to Bishop's Park off the Fulham Palace Road. Visit the palace built by Bishop Fitzjames. It features a selection of rare old trees and shrubs collected by Bishop Grindall. Don't tell anyone else though - it's our secret.

Old Man River

It was during the Tudor period at this time that Old Father Thames came into his own and became a major thoroughfare, with hundreds of watermen offering their services just like black cabs today. It's difficult to imagine now, when all you see is the odd pleasure cruiser or a lonely little river-police launch, that there were times when you could practically walk across the river from boat to boat. At one time there were so many boats that rowers had to raise their oars to pass each other. This, of course, gradually led to London spreading along the river's banks; catching up and absorbing villages like Chelsea, in a westerly direction, and Woolwich and Deptford, where Henry VIII built his royal dockyards, to the east.

Back to the Fuchsia

One of the oldest pubs in London is, believe it or not, still there. The Prospect of Whitby on Wapping Wall, was originally built in 1520 and was a haunt for smugglers and river pirates. For years it was known as the Devil's Tavern. *The Prospect* was a boat from Whitby which was moored nearby and it was from this that the pub took its name. In the early eighteenth century, a sailor in the pub sold a plant which he had managed to keep alive during his travels. It was the first fuchsia plant in the country.

By the Way

In 1481, a mysterious recurring disease called 'sweating sickness' arrived with foreign mercenaries who'd come over to Milford Haven with Henry Tudor. It was remarkable because it only seemed to affect the rich (and about time too!). Some called it 'Stop-Gallant', 'for there were some dancing in the Court at nine o'clock that were dead at eleven'. It finally disappeared in 1551.

By the Way

Can you believe it? Author John Stowe was already beginning to rant about the ruination of London in 1525 (the poor devil should see it now). He was forever banging on about when

London was all fields. God knows what he'd think if he could see all those little villages way out to the edges of Middlesex, that have now been sucked into one vast, three-up, two-down urban soup.

Despite the surge in population within the city, there were still pockets that remained pretty rural. Can you imagine that Leicester Square, the almost nightmarish centre for modern city life was still pastureland, and Soho, now all gay bars and poncy ad-person clubs, was to remain parkland for another century?

OK, DARLING—
SEE YOU IN THE
GROUCHO CLUB
IN 475 YEARS'
TIME

Reformation Time

Everyone in England was getting well hacked off with the hypocrisy of the Catholic Church. The hanky-panky that went on between the naughty nuns and the mischievous monks behind the high walls of their nunneries and monkeries, was a badly kept secret. The corruption of the clergy, especially the selling of indulgences (pardons) like ice lollies in a heatwave, provided them with sumptuous lifestyles. This really got up the noses of the English. Anyway, they pondered, what's the

TO WHOM IT MIGHT CONCERN

use of a religion in a different language (Latin)? That must be about as useful as a computer with no software.

Look Out, Luther's About

Cardinal Wolsey, Archbishop of York, didn't help. He was richer than even Henry VIII and rode out from his palace, smothered from head to foot in gold, to yell at the citizens of the dangers of German Protestant Martin Luther (the brains behind the Reformation). In 1516 Wolsey ordered the city folk (who hated him) to 'curtail the sedition, disobedience and disorders caused by vagabonds and "masterless folk" who roamed its streets.' This was met by that very familiar two-finger gesture that hailed from the Battle of Agincourt.*

'Evil May Day'

A year later, when trade was going through a rather shaky patch, the blame fell on foreign merchants. On May Day 1517, despite an evening curfew, a bunch of yobs followed by a mass of Londoners, broke into all the private prisons, released the grateful inmates and ransacked the houses of anyone with a slightly foreign-sounding name (there were about 4,000 registered in London). When it was all over, the ringleaders (called 'younglings') were rounded up, tried for treason, and promptly strung up. The rest were made to parade the streets with nooses round their necks. This action unfortunately led to the sympathetic natives hating foreigners even more.

* *The British longbow was so fast compared to the French crossbow that the archers would taunt the French with the two fingers used to pull the bow string back.*

By the Way

To save having to move the prisoners around the city, ten mobile gallows were built which trundled hither and thither providing a wonderful on-the-spot service - a bit like mobile libraries (well, a bit!).

Bang Go the Monasteries

By 1527, Henry VIII was in a tricky situation. He wanted to trade in his ugly old wife (Catherine of Aragon) for a nice shiny new one (Anne Boleyn), but the Pope wouldn't let him - spoilsport! Henry, who was anything but stupid, realised he'd have to make up and be friends with all those non-Catholics that he'd regarded as heretics before (and had been setting fire to on a regular basis).

But being the monarch has its advantages (well it used to). Using the quickly thought up Act of Supremacy, in 1531 he suddenly made himself head of the Church and in effect told the Catholics and their Pope exactly where they could shove their liturgy. He also made himself a cool fortune by snatching all the Church's vast wealth. Henry was never one to muck about and, to prove it, had a weird prophetess, Elizabeth Barton - nick-named the Holy Maid of Kent - executed. She had claimed that Henry would die a villain's death if he were to marry Anne. It just shows what could happen to anyone who disagreed with him. Actually, if Elizabeth had been any good at prophesising, she'd have forecast what would happen to her and kept her mouth shut.

By the Way

In 1532 a Franciscan monk also warned Henry against going

through with the divorce, saying that if he did, one day dogs would lick his blood as they had done Ahab's. In 1547 when Henry's stinking and corpulent body was stored overnight at Syon House, on the way to Windsor, the coffin lid burst open in the night and the dogs guarding it were found licking his remains in the morning. Spooky but true!

Be Warned

In 1537 five Catholic friars of the Charterhouse monastery, who refused to accept Henry as their new boss, met their end in a rather distasteful way. One at a time they were hanged at Tyburn but, before they became unconscious, were cut down so causing them further injury as they hit the ground. As if that wasn't bad enough, they were then laid on planks and had their stomachs cut open with a knife. Their innards were then drawn out in front of them, and they were finished off by having their hearts torn out. Now dead, they found themselves going in four directions at once (quartering). All this was supposed to have been a warning to others. Can't think why! The rest of the friars were imprisoned at Newgate, where they were shackled to the wall in order to have time to repent. They starved to death. Obviously no food for thought there.

By the Way

The Bishop of Rochester, John Fisher, was executed for not admitting to the supremacy of Henry, and his head was put up on the bridge. It was soon taken down some time later and thrown in the river because, instead of rotting, it was said to be looking better and better as the time wore on. (Sounds like Cliff Richard.)

By Another Way

Boiling in oil was legalised by Henry VIII in 1530, primarily for ladies who'd killed their husbands. They'd usually be strapped to a pole and dunked into a bubbling cauldron. The Bishop of Rochester's cook was, appropriately, the first to go in the pot (to try it out). What about Lloyd Grossman next?

I HOPE HE TASTES BETTER THAN THE SOUP HE MADE

There was obviously no need for Catholic monasteries (or monks) so they were disbanded. The problem was that all the monasteries throughout the country had been a source of labour and hand-outs for the rural poor, so yet another ragged group of peasants was stuck up a creek without a paddle, so to speak, and forced to join the ever growing river of people heading for the bright lights of London (well, candlelight actually). This included all the barmy and very old people who, up to this point, had always been cared for by monks and nuns.

Londoners watched in awe as all the monastic buildings were stripped and their religious valuables distributed (usually to Henry VIII's mates and courtiers). Even the buildings themselves were sold off and put to private use, and this started a massive property boom, probably the first to be seen in London. It could well have been the first we saw of another dreaded scourge that was to ravage London for the rest of time. No, not rats . . . estate agents!

By the Way

Henry VIII ordered the Countess of Salisbury to be executed because he couldn't wreak his vengeance on her son, Cardinal Pole. She refused to lay her head on the block because she thought it undignified, so the poor executioner had to chase after her and chop off her head while still running (good game, good game!). Apparently, on the anniversary of her death, this ghostly and grisly chase may still be observed.

Water Everywhere

With the population of London rising in leaps and bounds, there was a major problem - water. There just wasn't enough of it. A Dutch servant called Peter Morice came up with the answer - a ginormous waterwheel, built under the first arch of London Bridge, which pumped the clean (ish) river water through new lead pipes to the surrounding areas.

By the Way

Clever Morice issued a 500-year lease for his invention. The Metropolitan Water Board still holds the rights and has to pay £2.50 annually on each of the 1,500 shares that the present shareholders own, even though the whole system was scrapped centuries ago.

Bloody Mary

When Henry the VIII's boy, Edward VI, died, everyone who was doing all right in London breathed in hard. Big changes were ahead at the top. There had been a brief attempt to put the beautiful, but well-tragic, Lady Jane Grey on the throne, and for a short while (14 days) she was there.

By the Way
One little vintner's boy, on yelling 'long live Queen Mary', had his ears nailed to the nearest pillory, a classic case of the right comment at the wrong time.

But the average Briton, not too worried about what he said in church, or whose version of God he believed in, preferred to keep things legal, and Catholic Mary, the rightful heir, soon became Queen and Lady Jane became topless (well, headless) in the Tower. Queen Mary I was determined to get Britain back to how it had been before her dad put his big Anglican foot in it, and was also determined to hang, beat or burn anyone who got in her way.

Londoners, never ones to avoid a scrap, became the troops for the religious unrest. The long-suffering citizens had become almost used to the sad processions of those martyrs caught the wrong side of the religious fence, on their way to part company with various bits of their bodies. Eventually everyone was forced to take sides. This made it a very dodgy business, living in a country that was constantly switching its religious goalposts.

It was then that all the barbecuing (of Protestants) started in Smithfield on a regular basis. Fun for all the family.

Famous Londoners No. 6: *Thomas Gresham (1519-79)*

Young Thomas Gresham started as a gunpowder salesman but, through his genius for matters financial, became the main agent of the Crown, especially (later) for Elizabeth I, doing most of her buying and selling abroad. He was also her tame financial adviser. He thought up the still mentioned 'Gresham's Law' which says that 'bad money drives good money out of circulation'.

He'd been sorting out the young Edward VI's affairs when Edward died, letting 'Bloody' Mary I in. Like many people who'd been loyal to non-Catholics, he kept his head well down for a while, until she called him in to sort out the dog's breakfast that his successor had made of it. Mary kept him on until she herself died, paying him in large tracts of land plus 20 shillings a day. Not much? These days it would be nigh on £260 a day or £94,000 a year. Not bad – I say.

Gresham is most remembered for inventing the forerunner of the Stock Exchange. He thought it was totally daft for businessmen to have to stand around Lombard Street in the cold and rain to do business 'like pedlars', so he built London its first trading centre with his own cash. It was massive, and called 'the Royal Exchange'.

His magnificent building was decorated with carvings of grasshoppers (the carvings are still to be seen around the City). Gresham, like Whittington before him, really got off on the old 'poor boy made good' chestnut and claimed that, when little, he'd been abandoned in a field and it was only the chirping of the grasshoppers that had kept him from slipping into unconsciousness and dying. This story, like Whittington's, was pure baloney.

By the Way

In order to build his Exchange, Gresham destroyed eighty houses in four streets, without even asking the inhabitants.

The original Exchange buidling was frazzled in the Great Fire of 1666 but the present one, built in 1844, stands on the same site. During Gresham's lifetime, owing to the trouble Northern Europe was having from the pesky Spanish, London's Exchange became the world's new marketplace. Huge trading companies, like the Hudson Bay, the Guinea, the Muscovy, the Levant and, the largest, the East India Company set up trading networks throughout the known world. These were to become so powerful that they were often effective governments in many of their areas of influence.

Spanish Connection

Everything was going fine until Mary, thinking she was making a smart deal, announced she was going to marry Philip, the King of Spain. Sir Thomas Wyatt, a swashbuckling soldier, simply couldn't bear the Spanish and found 3,999 others who couldn't either. Together they marched from Kent (why were they always from Kent?) to London where Mary was a little nervous as most of her soldiers were . elsewhere.

('If only rebels gave one a little warning,' I expect she thought.) Luckily, thousands of the loyal folk of London rallied round and volunteered to help her.

When Wyatt got to London he found the bridge closed (surprise, surprise) so promptly took out his wrath on Southwark which, let's face it, everybody did. He then snuck down to Kingston that night and paddled across the river with most of his men. By two in the morning they'd come up the other side and reached Hyde Park Corner where poor old Mary only had 500 proper soldiers to meet them. By the following morning all the rebels were tearing up what's now the West End like football hooligans on Cup Final night. After trying to get at Mary (who'd been hiding in the Tower), Wyatt himself was captured in a fish shop and badly battered (geddit?).

By the Way

Sir Thomas Wyatt was beheaded on Tower Hill in 1542, much to the relief of his widow Mrs Wyatt, as he'd already given her eleven kids by the time he was thirty-three.

GOOD NEWS, KIDS — NO MORE KIDS!

★ WORTH A VISIT? ★

If you go to the western end of the gardens of Trinity Square, you'll find a small stone, set into the pavement, marking the exact spot of the execution site. The last people to die there were two prostitutes in 1780.

ELIZABETHAN LONDON

London, that monstrous tuberosity of civilised life: Thomas Carlisle

Elizabeth I, Mary's younger half-sister and product of the now three-quarter size Anne Boleyn (that's head removal for you) and Henry VIII, came to the throne in 1558. Not to be outdone, she had her cousin, Mary Queen of Scots, executed to bring peace to the country and nip rumours of a Spanish invasion (they wanted Catholic Mary) neatly in the bud. The London that this bizarre young queen lived in had reached one of the most fascinating and lurid periods in its history.

Swinging London No. 1 (see No. 2 page 240).

As you will have gathered from her sister Mary's antics (Protestant-burning and the like), human life counted for peanuts in those days and public executions had become a cheap day out for all the family. Very often at the weekends, your average Tudor family would have a choice of executions to go to, like choosing a movie or footer match.

BUT DAD PROMISED WE COULD SEE THE NUNS BURN

★ WORTH A VISIT? ★

If you have a fascination with fighting, especially with swords, try Hanging Sword Alley, in EC4, famous for fencing schools in the sixteenth century. It was also known as 'Blood Bowl

Alley' owing to a notoriously violent night-cellar made famous by the painter Hogarth.

Famous Londoners No. 7: *Edmund Campion*

In 1581, Edmund Campion, a Jesuit, was falsely accused of plotting against the state and put on the rack at the Tower. I don't know if he ever had any problems with his height, but he was reported to be ten centimetres taller when finally hanged.

By Elizabeth's time, it must be said, people were shown the red card for doing practically nothing. A break-in at Charterhouse Lane in 1558, for instance, in which a hankie worth twelve pence and a key worth eight pence were taken, ended up with the dastardly villain dangling decoratively on the end of a Newgate rope. Likewise, two wicked little rascals who pickpocketed five shillings at Marylebone could be seen swinging soulfully at Tyburn (now Marble Arch).

Luckily there was no shortage of people to hang. The number of beggars and destitutes had rocketed, largely due to Henry's closure of the monasteries (big job providers), and the crime (albeit petty) had soared in direct proportion. One Bridewell (coming soon) inmate, no doubt under pressure from a little light torture, confessed in 1576 that a gang of thieves gathered on Saturday night in a barn at Tothill Street, Westminster (now dead posh) and another met in a cowshed in Lambeth with 'diverse whores' (and diverse cows no doubt). This info resulted in many hangings, though I believe the cows were let off with a caution.

By the Way

In 1577 a certain John Sherwood was one of those honoured to reside in perhaps the worst prison in London, 'the dongeon amongst the ratts' at the Tower. It was a cave, way underground with no light, which had a nasty habit of being infested with rats every time the tide came up.

As well as all the gaols, compters and lock-ups, 'Houses of Correction' popped up all over London, designed to take the destitute men, women and children off the streets and set them to hard work – all ever so commendable stuff (if you're a fascist). Unfortunately these places were as good as prisons and one at Bridewell Palace, an old home of Henry VIII's, shoved the poor in with the thieves and prostitutes. As for the 'work', they often ended up walking treadmills all day or unpicking tarry ropes to make oakum (used to seal the bottoms of boats), in somewhat less than four-star conditions (no en-suite bathroom or trouser press).

By the Way

For years Bridewell's inmates had been regularly whipped so, to make the whole thing into much more of a spectator sport, the governors opened the show – sorry – proceedings, to the public, even constructing a gallery so they might get a better view. Residents would be stripped to the waist and the junior beadle★ would flog them for all they were worth (I can think of a certain Beadle I'd like to flog) until the President of the Court saw fit to strike the table with his hammer signalling the end.

★ *Officer appointed by the council.*

One of the other results of the closure of the monasteries was that all the poor sick (or the sick poor) were thrown out on the streets, and St Bartholomew's Hospital (Bart's), which is still going today (just) had to take in many more patients than it could possibly cater for. (So nothing's changed there then!)

By the Way

Bart's first physician, Dr Roderigo Lopez, was executed at Tyburn because Elizabeth reckoned he'd tried to poison her. But my theory is that it was really because he had a dodgy, Spanish-sounding name, and Elizabeth was on their hit list.

London Expands

London by the mid-1500s was growing at an enormous rate. John Stowe, a contemporary historian, thought it 'unpredictable and unstable - out of control'.

The East End had gradually become the poorest part of London, an honour it was to hold for the rest of its history (until the yuppies started moving in - in the late 1980s). Wealthier folk began moving west, but it's interesting to note that at that time, few were interested in the area south of the river. (It must be said that most North Londoners still aren't much interested in south of the river and vice-versa).

GOSH! THERE'S AN AWFUL LOT OF THEM

It was Queen Elizabeth herself who, on peeking over the city walls, noticed how overcrowded it was becoming and decreed that no new buildings should go up within three miles. This, like most radical planning ideas, had exactly the opposite effect. All that happened was that instead of people moving further out, development within the walls went haywire; either downwards – with extra cellars being dug; upwards – with crazy lofts piled on the top of existing buildings; or sideways with gardens and yards being simply built over, just so's they could cram in more people and make more loot. London was becoming a seething, smelly mass of grubby humanity, and conditions were so disgusting that even the rats were ringing their travel agents and packing their bags. Burials were to far outstrip baptisms right up till 1700.

When it was seen that the authorities could do nothing at all about the situation, the canny builders crept outside the walls again and began what became the great suburban infill. Having said that, however central you might be at any time in Tudor London, you still only had to walk for a relatively short distance before you were in open sheep-filled, bird-tweeting meadows and countryside that looked like Constable paintings (haywains, milkmaids etc). Names like St Giles-in-the-Fields or St Martin-in-the-Fields tell you that when these churches were first built, areas like Covent Garden or Trafalgar Square (where they are) were exactly that – in the fields.

Elizabethan Fun

Southwark was still where everything was happening fun-wise in the 1500s. You could go to one of the many pub-theatres with their galleried balconies round central courtyards. These were banned in 1574 – firstly because any large grouping of people was thought to encourage the spreading of the plague, and secondly because many, if not most of the plays performed, were judged to be too rude.

By the Way

The newly and stunningly rebuilt Globe Theatre is located on the same site as the original which had started life as, simply,

'The Theatre' at Clerkenwell (built there to avoid the city censorship). It was removed lock, stock and actors, right down to the last seat, when the lease ran out, which annoyed the ground landlords no end. Among the seven owners was a certain William Shakespeare who, I'm told, wrote things.

Animal Fun

Another great attraction loved by rich and poor alike, was that of watching animals tearing each other apart and betting on the results. There were several bear- or bull-baiting rings in Southwark. One could watch fierce, salivating mastiffs or greyhounds being pulled limb from limb by cross bears (who'd been blinded by their owners), or vice versa, tossed into the air by bulls or, occasionally, ripped to pieces by lions. Heigh-ho! John Evelyn the great London diarist went with friends to the Beare Gardens, as they were called, and wrote afterwards that 'one of the bulls tossed a dog full into a lady's lap, as she sat in one of the boxes at a considerable height from the arena. Two poor dogs were killed, and so all ended with the ape on horseback, and I most heartily weary of the rude and dirty pleasure'.

Bear-baiting, you'll be astonished to learn, was only finally banned in 1835, and cockfighting just a few years later.

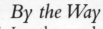

By the Way

In the early seventeenth century, drunken drovers would get their kicks from stampeding their cattle through the streets of London. The terrified animals would blunder into the wayside open-fronted shops, to get away from the blows and embarrassing bum-prods of the herdsmen. It is thought that this is the origin of the expression 'like a bull in a china shop'.

Football Fun

Don't go thinking that football hooliganism is a new invention. In 1586 the game was banned and three young men were imprisoned for 'outrageously and riotously behaving themselves at football play at Cheapside'.

★ WORTH A VISIT? ★

The Queen's Elm, a pub on Fulham Road, had been called 'The Queen's Tree' as far back as 1667. It was named such because Queen Elizabeth, on her way to somewhere or other (probably to watch Chelsea play at home), sheltered under an ancient elm nearby during a torrential storm.

In a Stew

The South Bank was still the main centre for all the whorehouses or 'stews', as they were known at the time. They were still concentrated on the land of the Bishop of Winchester (which is why the 'ladies' were nicknamed 'Winchester geese') and, to make sure everyone recognised them, they were painted in virginal white (not the whores – the houses), rather an odd choice of colour, I'd have thought. The most famous one was nick-named 'the Cardinal's Hatte' in deference to his lordship the Bishop. The Hatte was famous for its cuisine and high-flying clientele. Pepys observed much 'brabbling and fraying' – which meant public rowdyism and copulation.

But prostitution, though frowned on, was a profitable business for all concerned, especially the authorities, who received substantial licence fees (and were, without doubt, regular customers). Henry VIII closed all the Southwark stews owing to a nasty wave of syphilis in 1546 but, when he died a year later (probably from a nasty wave of syphilis), they reopened under the very short reign of the very short Edward VI. The prudish and pious Mary Tudor, as you might have guessed, closed them again but they were open for business as soon as Elizabeth became queen.

By the Way

If you're a student now, or ever have been, of the highly prestigious Alleyn's School or Dulwich College (once known as Alleyn's College of God's Gift at Dulwich), it might interest you to know where your eminent founder, Sir Edward Alleyn, got the money. He was not only a notorious brothel and bear garden keeper (he was 'Master of the Royal Game of Bears, Bulls and Mastiff Dogs') but, and much worse than all that, a well-known actor – far more disreputable.

Armada Ahoy

What's the Spanish Armada got to do with a book about London, I expect you're asking? Well, I bet if you caught wind of 130 mighty galleons, full of murderous Spaniards, chundering up the English Channel towards your home town, you might understand. In 1588 Philip II of Spain sent

La Flota Armada Invinceble to restore England to Catholicism (I'd have told them to - um - mind their own business), and to try and persuade the English fleet to stay away from its new American lands.

At the entrance to the Thames, at Tilbury, the English lashed 120 masts and 40 anchors together, which not only made a sort of bridge to mount their guns on, but was hopefully to be a ship-proof barrier. Further up, on all the river bends, was more artillery, placed so that it could catch the enemy broadside-on as they swung into view, and, lastly, a huge boom was put across the river at Blackwall (where the tunnel is now). As well as proper soldiers, 10,000 irregulars were raised and placed along the sides of the river. London was ready.

By the time the Queen came to review her troops, news came that the Spanish fleet had been well and truly trashed by a combination of our much littler, much nippier ships and the rest of the Spanish army simply not turning up to meet them at Calais. Tee hee!

STUART LONDON 1603-1714

London is chaos incorporated: George Mikes

Queen Elizabeth died (mad, bald, smelly and toothless) in the spring of 1603, letting in James VI of Scotland who became James I of England as well. He'd been left up in Scotland by his murderous mummy, Mary, when she had to disappear southwards a bit smartish, having been chased out for blowing up her husband (sounds reasonable).

It is reported that when he first drove through Lewisham on his way down to London (no mean feat - Lewisham's SOUTH of London), James thought that it was London itself and became quite excited (excited over Lewisham?). Actually, I think this said more about Scotland than Lewisham, but we won't pursue that now. On finally reaching London, which was by then ten times the size of any other English town, he seemed relatively unimpressed (not helped by yet another outbreak of the plague) and was only consoled when told he'd be King of Lewisham as well. BIG DEAL! (sorry Lewisham).

HI! LEWISHAM

By the Way

Londoners were dying to catch a glimpse of their new king, but were to be sorely disappointed. James was terrified of the plague and cut himself off in his favourite palace at Whitehall which he made into a hotbed of drinking and gay frolics (literally). When a courtier told him that he really should make more of an effort (with his subjects I hasten to add), he yelled 'God's wound! I will pull down my breeches and they shall also see my arse!' He absolutely hated these new Londoners, you see. The Queen, by the way, moved her court up the road to Denmark House – and who can blame her?

Water Worries

The poor old Thames was struggling under the strain of all that was expected of her. Not only did she have to provide transport for the citizens, but also allow foreign shipping to come right into the heart of London. On top of all that, she had to supply the whole of central London with water to wash in, cook in and most important of all – drink. But with all the human and animal 'by-products', and the increasing amount of light industrial waste pouring into her, she was fast becoming an open sewer. In those days they didn't even know

how to begin to treat water. Not only that, but the natural wells at Goswell and Clerkenwell had also become mucky. Water had to be found somewhere else.

A New River

What they wanted was a new clean source of water, and they

realised that if you haven't got one, you've gotta make one. From Elizabethan times there had been a plan to cut a brand new river (called, surprisingly, 'the New River') from way out in Hertfordshire. But the entrepreneurs kept running out of that other liquid commodity – money. Eventually in 1613, thanks to a large contribution from the otherwise useless King James, a channel was dug three metres wide and one metre deep for over thirty-eight miles (no mean feat with only buckets and spades). This stream deposited the valuable H_2O in a vast reservoir in Clerkenwell. From the 'New River Head', as it was called, water was pumped into the city by pipes made of wood or leather, though Londoners from the very start severely mistrusted this new 'foreign' water. Mind you, anything had to be better than the human 'soup' they'd been sucking out of the Thames.

★ WORTH A VISIT? ★

Later in the seventeenth century, the New River (now somewhat wider) became a favourite place for anglers. Eels caught in the river were served at the famous Eel Pie House, a tavern at Highbury famous for its pies and rat-killing matches, where there was also a little wooden house astride the river. This diverted some of the flow to provide water for Holloway. To find the site, go to 57 Wilberforce Rd, Islington, but don't tell 'em I sent you.

By the Way

Talking of rivers, in 1624 Cornelius Drebbel, the Duch tutor to James I's kids, invented the first submarine. It was powered by twelve oarsmen who rowed between Westminster and Greenwich bridges. Even King James had a go in it.

Freezing Up

One of the other great problems of having a river clogged with refuse was that it made it run much more slowly, especially around London Bridge. There all the debris got snarled up on the massive pillars, so causing it to freeze over as soon as the weather turned chilly. In 1608 a 'Frost Fair' was held for the first time. Suddenly there was a vast area of undeveloped land (well, ice) to use purely for pleasure – everything from impromptu ox-roasts, football pitches (football on ice?), even souvenir printing presses. It seems difficult to imagine, but the Frost Fairs continued until 1831 when the old London Bridge was pulled down and the river went back to full speed ahead once more.

Having the river frozen caused no end of a problem for transport, especially for the watermen who lost their income. They got round the problem by cutting a channel between the bank and the ice and charging people to cross over it. But the watermen had worse to come. When someone in 1625 invented the very first land-based hackney carriage (the horse-drawn forerunner of the taxi) the writing was on their wall. Watermen were soon to complain of their profits 'running away on wheels'. In a relatively short time, just like the poor old Thames, the narrow city streets were clogged with hackney carriages, sedan chairs, private landaus and huge, rickety stage-wagons (the equivalent of lorries). At all the entrances to the city were hundreds of stagecoaches falling over each other to take people to far-flung towns and cities.

Westward Ho

London was creeping further and further westward and the West End (these days regarded as the centre) was established for all the snobbish, wealthy people who were beginning to get tired of living near and around 'men in trade'.

Guy Fawkes

The infamous and Catholic Guy Fawkes and his men probably hated James and his parliament more than most. Following a tip-off, magistrate Sir Thomas Knyvert went down into the crypt under the Peers' Chamber at the Houses of Parliament on 5th November 1605 and found the poor guy (Guy) standing next to a ton and a half of gunpowder with the fuses in his hand (tricky sitch - eh!). When asked exactly what he was doing there, Guy, with characteristic good humour, quipped 'one of my objects was to blow Scotsmen back to Scotland'. Trouble was, his interrogators didn't really get the joke and poor Mr Fawkes underwent some of the worstest torture known to man - for three days. This included such joys as being stretched on the rack (he was tall anyway), hanged, drawn and quartered. The custom of children collecting money for a stuffed effigy comes from the ancient rhyme:

Penny for the Guy
Hit him in the eye
Stick him up a lamp post
And there let him die.

Inigo Jones

Inigo Jones, perhaps London's, England's and maybe the world's, greatest architect, was born in London but spent many years poring over, and making little drawings of, the fab buildings in Italy. In 1615 he came back to the old country and was made the King's Surveyor. He was a workaholic and committed himself to hundreds of projects many of which, believe it or not, are still standing. Easiest of all to see now is St Paul's Church at one end of the piazza at Covent Garden (just behind the street performers), the last remaining piece of his original plan.

★ WORTH A VISIT? ★

There's also a bar-cum-restaurant-cum-club called the Rock Garden in the piazza at Covent Garden. It stands on the site of the old Tavistock Hotel, perhaps the finest house Inigo Jones ever built (demolished in 1928). If you go upstairs to the snack room, you'll be in the exact location of the infamous 'disreputable bedrooms' used by prostitutes and actresses (often the same thing in those days).

★ WORTH ANOTHER VISIT? ★

You might also like the Queen's House, part of the Maritime Museum at Greenwich, built by Jones for James's poor, frustrated missis (it's no fun having a gay husband apparently). It was the first really Palladian (Italian-style) bit of architecture in London. Inigo Jones believed that a building should follow three basic rules - 'masculine, solid and simple' (just like Frank Bruno).

Leave Us Alone

In 1617 James I issued the most extraordinary edict. He said that any gentleman who didn't own a town house in London, should get out and live at his country estate.

Presumably if you didn't have either, you couldn't even be a proper gentleman. This made many of the best families in England very anti-Royal and, for the first time since the Wars of the Roses, the king and his huge entourage of Scottish hangers-on had numerous enemies both in the Lords and the Commons.

James, undaunted, then went on to hack off the London merchants, who'd been more or less doing their own thing with huge success for years without having monarchs sticking their aristocratic noses into their business. There they were, in the middle of a commercial revolution, with the Crown trying to muscle in on the action. Shareholders in the aforementioned Russia, Muscovy and East India Companies were pulling their corporate hair out at the way the Crown delivered mixed messages while they were continually attempting to line their own pockets. By the time James died, Londoners were completely fed up with the old poof and his bestest favourite 'sweet Steenie' (the young, camp Duke of Buckingham) his, and his son Charles's, favourite courtier.

By the Way

James was one of the very first anti-smoking campaigners. He banned it from the palace, claiming it ruined men's sweet breath (hmmmm!). He further proved it by removing the head of Sir Walter Raleigh who brought tobacco here in the  first place. He also banned golf, claiming it was taking his archers away from their practice. He didn't even mention how boring it was.

Civil War

What's the first two things you don't do to an increasingly Puritan country if you want to become popular? Answer – marry a Catholic or a Frenchwoman. Charles I (James's boy) did both in an almost calculated attempt to outdo his dad in finding ways to really annoy his subjects. On top of that, his Queen had brought over hundreds of her nearest and dearest from Catholic France, who proceeded to freeload at the expense of the already fuming citizens of London.

WHERE'S THE TOAST?

By the Way

Madame de St Georges, the Queen's best mate, hated English food, and chucked her full English breakfast out of the window and down into the Strand. Before long, a crowd had gathered yelling, 'Death to the Papists'. A slight over-reaction on both sides, if you ask me.

Things got so bad that in the end it all ended in a nice new Civil War between the Puritan 'Roundheads' under Cromwell and the Royalist 'Cavaliers' under Charles. The Puritans, who'd been getting stronger and stronger in London, reckoned that the city was becoming riddled with the following bad practices:

'Idolatry, superstition, woeful profaning of the names, titles, attributes, creatures, and of God himself, with the perfect language of the hellish swearers in every child's mouth, whoredoms, adulteries, fornication, murders, oppressions, drunkenness, cozening [cheating], lying, the contempt of the Gospel with slandering, mocking, flouting, chiding,

silencing and stopping the mouths of God's prophets and servants, and other gross secret sins.

- which certainly isn't bad for starters.

By the Way

In 1650 it was ordained that 'common bawds [prostitutes] should be whipp'd openly and branded with a B on the forehead'. (Fine if your name was Beryl.) For each whipping, the keeper of the prison received fourpence.

London's Civil War began in 1642 and, although everyone was dead nervous, no actual battles took place nearer than Brentford (which is out past Kew). The only real effect the war had was a downturn in trade and the occasional shenanigans of unpaid soldiers rampaging through the streets.

Charles's soldiers were even worse off than the Roundheads (Parliamentarians), as he was as good as stony broke. The only money Charles could raise was by selling off his land and property real cheap which was how many of the richest property owners in Britain today started off. At least the Roundheads had Parliament, which continued to get a fat income from the City, on their side.

London Looks Out

The Royalists, who were based at Oxford, rather surprisingly, completely trounced the Parliamentarians at Brentford, and poor old London suddenly had to think about defending itself. When the Royalists marched to Turnham Green, however (no tube station in those days I'm afraid), they were gobsmacked at the huge numbers (24,000) of artillery and pikemen who had been mustered to defend London. So Charles sloped away to Kingston to think it over.

The main advance on the city came in 1643, when the Royalists were due to be met by an elaborate system of trenches and ramparts, including twenty forts full of surly soldiers (3,000 in sum) surrounding the city, thrown up in the last year by every man, woman and child in London. It had fast become the best defended city in Europe.

THIS SHOULD KEEP HIM OUT

It was a bit of a waste, really, as the attack never actually happened and in a couple of years hardly a trace remained of all their hard work. King Charles and his lads had been beaten in an out-of-town battle.

Cromwell Wins

By 1647 the Civil War was as good as won by the Parliamentarians. London was under martial law and everyone realised that there could never be peace while poor Charlie lived. He was arrested in 1648 and brought by river from Windsor.

Charles Gets His

On the day of his execution in 1649, the pint-sized king (he was barely five feet tall before losing his head) walked to the scaffold wearing two shirts, afraid that the multitude would think him shivering from fear. Whitehall was packed with faces at every window, people even scrambling on roofs and up trees to get a view of their king's last minutes. The last word he muttered to the executioner before the axe came down was reported to be 'Remember!' Remember what? I reckon it was part of something longer, like 'remember to feed the cat'. Who knows? All we know is that a desperate groan went through the crowd as they realised the horror of what they'd done.

Puritanism was to have its head for a few years, but it was so bloody miserable that few were sorry when the Restoration (of the monarch) came along.

BEG PARDON! YOUR MAJESTY

By the Way

Two bits of Charles's body were stolen from his tomb. The first, a vertebrae, was used as an ornamental salt cellar by physician Sir Henry Hertford (until Queen Victoria ordered him to put it back) and the second, a finger, was nicked by a workman who made it into a handle for his penknife. I suppose it's nice to still be useful after you're dead.

SHORT-LIVED FUN:
THE RESTORATION AND BEYOND

Nobody is healthy in London, nobody can be: Jane Austen

England and London were fed up with the Civil War and were even becoming a little weary of the endless Royalist executions that followed it. (You really can have too much of a bad thing.) As for life under Cromwell, the poor Londoners had almost forgotten how to smile. When they heard in 1660 that the monarchy was about to be restored and the fun-loving, but child-scaringly ugly, Charles II★ was on his way home from France, everyone pulled out their glad rags and set about some serious partying. Life under Cromwell and those Puritans had been bloody awful.

As he approached the city from the south coast, Charles caught a chorus of every available church bell ringing in his aristocratic ears (which might well have put some people off). He was met by a singing, cheering multitude as he crossed over London Bridge. John Evelyn, the diary writer, described the scene thus:

. . . above 20,000 horse and foot [soldiers], brandishing their swords and shouting with inexpressible joy, the ways strew'd with flowers, the bells ringing, the streets hung with tapestry, fountains running with wine . . . the windows well set with ladies; trumpets and music.

★ *He looked remarkably like the spaniel named after him.*

118

Charles was certainly out to have a good time and the 'Merrie Monarch', as he was tagged, encouraged writers, playwrights, musicians and all kinds of entertainers to help gee-up a city brought to its knees by years of political punch-ups. The period that followed was called 'The Restoration'. Charles even opened up his own redesigned St James's Park to the public and released newly imported ornamental ducks on the pond for the first time.

By the Way
Charles II was dead proud of having introduced the very first pelicans to the Park and England, and they drew amazed crowds. John Evelyn described them as 'melancholy waterfoul, brought from Astracan by the Russian Ambassador'.

Rude Rules
When the theatres were re-opened in 1666 there was a rush of highly sexy plays and rude comedies. Just what the repressed public wanted.

Houses were built all along Pall Mall, a street named after the wacky French game Paille Maille (a cross between croquet and golf)*. Charles's bestest girlfriend, the actress and former orange salesperson, Nell Gwynne, had been bought a house there (No. 79) and found she could chat to her boyfriend (and king) over his garden wall. Nell was, by all accounts, the seventeenth-century equivalent of a Page 3 Girl – but with a brain. To this day, No. 79 remains the only site (where the Eagle Star building sits) on the south side of the road not owned by the Crown. Clever Miss Gwynne insisted on the freehold because, as she wittily quipped, 'she'd always conveyed free under the Crown'.

*And played there before the Civil War.

By the Way

Nell Gwynne expressed a desire to be buried at St Martin-in-the-Fields (at the end of her street), but when she got there they couldn't think where to put her body. Thousands turned up at her funeral, but poor Nelly hung around for ages until the vicar, who must also have fancied her (though in a rather macabre way), decided she could be put in his own personal vault.

★ WORTH A VISIT? ★

You can visit the amazing vaulted crypt any day for free. There you'll find a large café and the fascinating Brass Rubbing Centre in which you can take rubbings from some of the finest European and Celtic church brasses around.

Despite being hitched to the dead prim and proper Catherine of Braganza (of Spain), Charles also encouraged all the other women round him to share his bedtime frolics. He ended up with no less than forty acknowledged royal bastards from thirteen known-about mistresses – and a load who weren't (imagine explaining all them to the wife). For five years London was to be a centre of light-hearted revelry until . . .

The Great Plague

. . .until, to the delight of all those pious, Puritan grumps who hadn't had a good Restoration, the last and by far the biggest outbreak of the plague since the Black Death, erupted in the unbearably hot summer of 1665. It was London's twentieth plague since AD 952 and it began in the slums of St Giles, Holborn, Finsbury, Whitechapel and Southwark. The Puritans, of course, said it had been sent by God to punish Londoners for smiling too much, but we all know that, once again, those horrid, disease-carrying, dirty rats had decided to set up home with all the pigs and poultry kept by most of the poor in their back yards. The Londoners, suspicious as ever, blamed the disease on Dutch visitors.

By the Way

One of the most popular of the thousands of old (mostly dead) wives' tales was that catching the plague could be avoided by regularly swilling the mouth out with vinegar. Smoking tobacco was also reckoned to be good for it. (That's a change.)

Slowly Does It

The epidemic started gradually, owing to the bitter weather, but when it warmed up (plagues love to be cosy) the disease spread like an ice cream dropped on a hot pavement. Rich people, remembering what had happened the last time round, thought, 'Blow this', and hightailed it back to their country estates. Soon there wasn't a doctor, priest, lawyer or judge to be found, which was not a load of fun if you were ill (or were going to be) or in need of a prayer, but brilliant if you were a villain. (There were no executions for six months.)

By the Way

If you want to read the very best account of the plague and what followed, try the wonderful diaries of Samuel Pepys (one of the few toffs who stayed behind). You won't find 'em boring – I promise.

By mid-July the survivors were burying 1,000 Londoners a week. But that was nothing; September saw the demise of 7,000 men, women and children.

By the Way

Close to the junction of what is now New Oxford Street and Tottenham Court Road (just by the monstrous Centre Point) scores of families were dying, and flies and ants not only covered the walls but were thick in the air.

Red Cross

If there was a hint of illness in a house, the whole family would be forced to nip down to the shops and would then be locked indoors for forty days, with a nice red cross on the door. Few ever came out alive. Smarter people enforced a kind of quarantine on themselves by moving onto makeshift houseboats in the middle of the Thames, which apparently helped. All the towns around the city locked their gates to prevent those fleeing from London from joining them. If Londoners did break in, it was not uncommon for them to be murdered or at least asked to leave in none too pleasant a manner.

By the Way

At the height of the panic, plague victims could be seen running stark naked through the streets or standing at their windows. They had mad eyes and were usually foaming at the mouth (sounds like a rave). Every pet pooch and pussy (400,000 and 200,000 respectively) was put down, as they were thought to be carriers of the disease (which, of course, they weren't).

Ghost City

By the time the cold weather came and the death rate started to drop, London had become like a ghost town in a cowboy film, with the carcasses of dead animals littering the walkways, and grass growing where the streets had once teemed with the hurly-burly of city life.

By now all the shops and restaurants were shut (except, of course, MacDonald's) and the only sounds to be heard were the cries of watchmen calling for the terrified residents to bring out their dead rellies (and pets), or the rattle of carts, carrying the ex-Londoners over the smoke-filled* cobbled streets. It's hard to imagine what it must have been like. Blimey, we make a fuss about a mild flu epidemic. Sometimes the poor devils leading the horse-drawn carts would collapse on the way to the burial pits and the horses, having no AtoZs (or brains) to help them find their way, would wander aimless and leaderless, pulling their grim cargo hither and thither wherever they fancied.

By the Way

On 31st July 1665 there was an ad in the *Intelligencer* that proclaimed that a certain William Boghurst, an apothecary at the White Hart in St Giles-in-the-Fields, was treating up to sixty patients a day. He had amazing success with his special medicines (eight pence an ounce). He also did home visits at very reasonable terms.

★ Worth a Visit? ★

If you want a great but grim reminder of the plague, go visit St Olaves Church in Seething Lane EC3. The gateway, built

---

* *Fires were lit everywhere because smoke was thought to purify the air - which it didn't, of course.*

shortly after the plague, bears five grisly sculptured skulls and a load of old bones. Buried there is Mary Ramsay, the woman blamed by many for bringing the plague to London, and also Mother Goose, a strange old crone who wrote the stories that were later transformed into the pantos *Puss in Boots* and *Cinderella*.

The plague eventually burned itself out having destroyed half of London's population. But, just as the poor Londoners were beginning to see the light at the end of the tunnel, another sort of light dealt them yet another fateful blow.

Fire!

It appears that an absent-minded baker called Thomas Faryner, in Pudding Lane EC3, forgot to damp down his oven one night in 1666 and so lit the worst fire that anyone had ever seen. Others say that a 'fat boy', while attempting to steal a pie from the baker's, scattered some coals. His statue now adorns the wall of the house at the corner (called Pie Corner) of Cock Lane (which, incidentally and appropriately, was the only licensed walk for prostitutes in the fourteenth century).

All those grumpy Godly folk, of course, insisted again that it was payment for those riotous good times, but the truth was that the dark, stinking, tangled alleys of almost-touching wooden buildings were nothing less than a ginormous bonfire waiting to happen. In minutes the Great Fire had swept up Thames Street (hungrily devouring its warehouses filled with oil, tallow, pitch, brimstone, hemp and lots of strong spirits), and on to London Bridge.

The streets soon became choked not only with acrid smoke, but with every single city dweller either trying to put the fire out (King Charles II, in all his satin and lace finery, joined in the thick of it) or stumbling about endeavouring to get his or her goods as far as possible from the heat.

By the Way

At one point the heat got so intense that the stones of St Paul's glowed red and the lead from the roof ran down the wall. Even more amazing, the heat cracked the tomb of Robert Braybrook, the very ex-Bishop of London (250 years ex) and the poor old stiff was catapulted into the churchyard. Crowds gathered to have a peep, and Samuel Pepys commented that his skin (he still had flesh), was 'tough, like spongy dry old leather'. Crikey, I know live people with skin like that.

At its peak, the fire could be seen from a distance of forty miles, lighting up the dark skies for many nights. Fortunes were made by looters and pickpockets and, as always in times of severe crisis, the inevitable unscrupulous spivs (early Del Boys) rented out horses and carts at ludicrously inflated prices. Business was business, I suppose.

By the Way

The Lord Mayor, Sir Thomas Bludworth, a bit of a silly arse by all accounts, instead of taking matters in hand by pulling down or blowing up houses to create fire-breaks, was rather unimpressed at the very beginning and was heard to remark, 'Pish, a woman might piss it out'. Some woman!

The fire blew out on the 6th of September, having burned over four fifths of the buildings within the city walls to the ground -13,000 houses, 87 churches, 4 prisons (and a rather insignificant baker's shop). Rather uncharacteristically, most prisoners had been let out prior to their temporary homes being engulfed in flames. The good news was that few people had been killed unlike the last fire of 1212, when over 1,000 men, women and children perished.

By the Way

Quite large hoards of money are still occasionally found in or around the city and are thought to have been buried (and then lost) all that time ago, in the panic as the fire approached.

Sleeping Out

OK, hardly anyone was killed (eight to be precise), but thousands upon thousands were left homeless (these days we manage that with our government housing policies). In Highgate alone, 200,000 camped in the fields. Although John Evelyn was heard to comment that London was destroyed, it's fair to say that it was only really the still largely medieval city that was done for. The nightmare of winding, gloomy, stinking wooden streets that had grown like an unplanned rat's nest were gone - reduced to a pile of smoking ashes. The other good news was that the fire had wiped out, once and for all, the accumulated filth of centuries, and disinfected the very soil that London sat upon. Plague was never to be a major problem again.

By the Way

An attention-seeking Frenchman called Robert Hubert confessed that he'd started the fire. Neither the judges nor Charles II really believed him, but they hanged the fool anyway (probably because he was French, Catholic - and very silly). It turned out later that he hadn't even been in London when the fire started.

What Now?

Five days after the main fire had gone out (it smouldered on for months), Christopher Wren, our other greatest architect in history, shoved one of a few mammoth plans for the rebuilding of London in front of the King (come to think of it, I reckon Chris might have started the fire). Had his scheme been accepted, it would have made London one of the most beautiful cities in the world, but the merchants and traders said, 'No way'. They were desperate to get back to business and couldn't wait for such an expensive operation. Anyway, winter was approaching and those wretched homeless had to be housed pretty damn quick.

Fire Works

Actually, having your city totally destroyed by a Great Fire isn't as bad as it sounds (but please don't try this at home). Just like all those German cities that were flattened in the Second World War and were rebuilt nice and modern-like, the upside was that Londoners had a chance to start almost completely from scratch and build a properly planned city. (What went wrong? I hear you ask.) At last, in 1667, a layout could be drawn up with proper building regulations, unlike the chaos that had gone before.

★ WORTH A VISIT? ★

If you're feeling fit you can still climb the tall Monument, built by Christopher Wren (with a little help from his friends) on the corner of Fish Street and Monument Street to commemorate the Great Fire. The view is well worth the near seizure. And so it should be. It's the tallest stone column in the world, and its sixty-six metres height is exactly the distance between where the Monument stands and where the fire started in Pudding Lane. The whole thing cost £13,450 11s 9d (nearly a million today). It carried an inscription falsely blaming the poor old Roman Catholics for the fire – 'in order for carrying on their horrid plott for extirpating the Protestant and old English liberty, and introducing Popery and Slavery' (steady on chaps).

EARLY BUNGEE JUMPING (WITHOUT BUNGEE)

By the Way

Rather appropriately, the first person to fling himself off the top of the tower was a baker. He was instant 'brown bread' (Cockney rhyming slang for 'dead'), of course.

Keep 'em Low

It was at this time that most of the now very old bits of London that we know and love today, came to be built. In the main streets the buildings had to be four storeys high and in the others no more than two. They were to be of brick and stone for obvious reasons, and the roads were cambered so that all the water and muck drained to the sides instead of staying in the centre. Most important of all, upper storeys were not allowed to jut out over the new streets which were now to be at least four metres wide. Huge markets were built to take the bulk of the trading off the streets.

One of the many problems of having no money is that you don't get to choose an awful lot. As usual, the poorest Londoners got the filthy end of the stick being squeezed into areas like Spitalfields and Tower Hamlets where the rents were much lower. The better-off merchant classes continued to move to the ever-growing and more  salubrious developments in West London, for no better reason than to get away from the growing menace of pollution, street violence . . . and those awful common people.

The mega-rich and trendy, who had hitherto chosen areas like Covent Garden and Lincoln's Inn Fields, now found them a bit too down-market and moved to Bloomsbury and the streets round St James's and Golden Squares. The huge building boom of 1713 was to give them rich ghettos like Mayfair and her surrounding squares. To be honest, they've never really changed.

One of the great money-making ideas had arrived in the

early 1660s when the Earl of Southampton invented the leasehold. At Bloomsbury Square he'd divided the land into small parcels and leased them out individually for a period of forty-two years. Developers leapt on the idea, realising that the narrower they could build, the more money they could make. Best of all, the actual landowner still held on to the land after the period of the lease. The fattest cats in London (mostly royalty) had at last found a slick, safe way of capitalising on all the land they owned.

Churches Again

The most important aspect of the rebuilding was the commission of fifty-two new churches (many standing today), all under Wren's guidance and sprinkled equally around the city. Plus, of course, the fab St Paul's Cathedral. This magnificent building was named after your actual St Paul (the Biblical superstar), who was supposed to have visited Britain on his world tour during Boudicca's time. The building of St Paul's took so long that by 1697 Parliament decided that Wren was taking everyone for a ride. They accused him of 'corruption and wilful delay', cutting his salary of £200 (£15,000 now) a year in half. The Cathedral was finally completed in 1710.

★ WORTH A VISIT? ★

If you want to see another nice Wren Church, try St Brides (the journalists' church) just off Fleet Street, rebuilt after the Great Fire. It's a little-known fact that its spire, made of four arched octagons reducing in size, gave pastrycook, Mr Rich, the idea for the first-ever tiered wedding cake! Bet he wished he was on a royalty.

By the Way

In 1667 the Fleet River was made into a canal between Holborn and Blackfriars so that it could take larger boats. Thirty years later it was so disgustingly smelly and clogged up with ... guess what, that they put it underground. The arches to the old Fleet Bridge are only a couple of feet underground at Ludgate Circus.

Famous Londoners No. 9: *Colonel Blood*

One of the most colourful characters of the time was the villainous-looking Colonel Thomas Blood who lived at the now demolished Bowling Alley (near Smith Square). His dastardly crimes included the attempted murder of the Duke of Ormonde in St James's Street and an assassination attempt on King Charles when he was bathing in the Thames at Battersea.

He was most remembered, however, for his attempt to steal the crown jewels in 1671. Blood had made friends (while dressed as a parson) with Talbot Edwards, who was in charge of looking after the jewels in the Martin Tower at the Tower of London. The charming colonel was invited to dinner by Edwards and his wife and, while being shown the jewels, threw a cloak over his host's head and clubbed him unconscious (great guest!). Blood, as he let his accomplices in, was disturbed by the keeper's soldier son who gave chase and captured the thieves at gunpoint before they could get to their getaway horses.

Blood was obviously a smooth talker for, instead of being hanged (or worse), he was personally interviewed by the King (whom he'd once tried to kill) and not only pardoned, but given back his forfeited lands in Ireland.

Famous Londoners No. 10: *Claude Duval*

Platt's Lane in Hampstead was once known as Duval Lane, after the swashbuckling and brilliant French highwayman, Claude Duval. It was named after him following a robbery in which he relieved a lady of her purse (containing £400) while she was riding in her carriage across the Heath. The lady in question, whilst being robbed, played sweetly on the flageolet as her furious husband looked on. Duval, charmed by her performance, only took £100.

Duval was arrested at the Hole in the Wall pub (now the Marquess of Granby) in Bedfordbury in 1670 and hanged at Tyburn, despite huge protestations by all the ladies who had fallen under his spell. His body lay in state at the notorious Tangier Tavern, before being taken to a funeral at St Paul's, Covent Garden. His stone read:

Here lies Du Valle: Reader, if man thou art, look to thy purse:
if female, to thy heart.

★ WORTH A VISIT? ★

If you're in Covent Garden, take a walk to Rose Street (off Garrick Street) where you will find the ancient Lamb and Flag Inn. On his way home from this local in 1679, the poet Dryden was set on by three cut-throats who called him a rogue and the son of a whore (which doesn't even rhyme) before beating him up. The man behind it was likely to have been the disgusting Earl of Rochester, a bisexual, worn out at thirty-two by a life of foul debauchery. He procured women for Charles II. (Honestly! They were all at it in those days!) Dryden had just ended their friendship, as he thought Rochester far too dangerous to know.

By the Way

There used to be a rather unusual club in Grub Street, Cripplegate. Members of the Farting Club would meet to compete with each other to produce the loudest and longest farts. Three guesses what they had for supper.

Famous Londoners No. 11: *Titus Oates*

One of London's most infamous characters was the rascal Titus Oates. He'd been expelled from Merchant Taylors School (still going strong) and was 'sent down' from Cambridge without a degree. Oddly enough, he managed to become a curate at All Saints, Hastings but was thrown in gaol for falsely trumping up a charge of sodomy against a local schoolmaster. On escaping he became chaplain on a boat bound for Tangier but was chucked off for doing exactly the same thing as he'd charged the other guy with – to a sailor. Someone who knew him described him as 'a most consummate cheat, blasphemer, vicious perjurer, impudent and foul mouthed wretch'. (I don't think he liked him.) Oates rose to fame in 1668 by hatching up a vicious lie to discredit the Catholics (which wasn't difficult in those days). He claimed that there was a plot to shoot poor Charles (with silver bullets, no less) when out with his spaniels in St James's Park, so that he could be replaced by the Catholic Duke of York.

Then, while recovering from a nasty dose of the clap, in his lodgings off Drury Lane, Oates made up an even better story that implicated Spanish Catholics, French Benedictines and a load of Irish and English people who'd voiced some disapproval of the King.

All in all, thirty-five totally innocent people were executed on his say-so. Titus was finally arrested at the Amsterdam Coffee House (behind the Royal Exchange). He was stripped of his church vestments and whipped 3,000 times all the way from Aldgate to Tyburn (and he wasn't even given the time to finish his coffee).

By the Way

Cat-lovers, look away! On one occasion 100,000 of Oates's followers met in Smithfield to burn an effigy of the Pope. To liven things up a little they stuffed it with live cats who screamed and squealed as they went up in flames.

By Another Way

Despite being imprisoned and kept shackled in irons, Oates managed to get the prison bedmaker pregnant. Also, despite a life sentence, he was released by William of Orange, granted a pardon and given a pension of ten quid a week. He died in 1704 in Axe Yard (now gone), a small street in Westminster (behind Downing Street).

I SUPPOSE YOU THINK YOU'RE VERY CLEVER, MR OATES

LONDON TAKES A DRINK

London is too full of fogs - and serious people. Whether the fogs produce the serious people or whether the serious people produce the fogs, I don't know, but the whole thing rather gets on my nerves:
Oscar Wilde 1892

Bye-Bye Charlie

Charles died in 1685, leaving a relatively happy country (and an even happier wife). His last words were 'Let not poor Nelly starve', referring to Nell Gwynne. He was replaced by the hated James II, his brother, which created instant problems as the English also hated Catholics with a passion – and he just happened to be one. His attempt to convert the whole country led to a bloodless revolution in 1688 and his replacement by Dutchman William of Orange and his goodly Protestant wife Mary (James's daughter). Mary was the real heir to the throne, and really popular. Her dad, by the way, ran away to France.

MR AND MRS W. ORANGE

Plain Annie

The eighteenth century opened with a new queen, Anne, younger daughter of James II. Poor old Anne didn't have much going for her (if you don't count being Queen). She was dull, obstinate and had a face that could turn milk. By the time she came to the throne in 1702, aged 37, she'd been pregnant a stupendous eighteen times, but only five children survived and they simply died as babies. (I suppose she deserves some credit for persistence.)

The Seedier Side

If for one moment I've given the impression that London was becoming a brighter and more respectable place to live, forget it. If anything, it was becoming much, much worse. It hit rock bottom in the mid-eighteenth century, owing to the mass of rough, tough soldiers and sailors who'd arrived home from fighting foreign foes, with no work and therefore no visible means of support.

The Duke of Marlborough's lot brought back a strange new drink, from the Netherlands, ominously called genievre (gin)*, that was to take London by storm before bringing it to its knees (literally).

Gin Mania

Drinking spirits had already gripped London's common folk as a relief from their grinding poverty, but up to then brandy had been their favourite tipple. The trouble was that it was a bit pricey compared to this new genievre (gin). Gin was a doddle to distil with the simplest of equipment and that's where all the trouble started. Grocers and shopkeepers didn't need a second chance at making their own brands, and competed with all the alehouses and inns, who were tied by the short and curlies to government licences. These gin shops openly used the slogan, 'drunk for a penny and dead drunk for tuppence. Clean straw to lie on.'

At first the government seemed all for it, and, in practically no time, gin and 'dram' shops seemed to have multiplied like flies on an old pork chop. At the height of the fun, there were over 6,000 establishments in London.

* From the French 'genevrier' or juniper berry (main constituent of gin).

All of a sudden the gin shops were more trouble than all the inns and alehouses put together (then doubled), but the government seemed deaf to what the magistrates were telling them. Eventually the epidemic nearly brought the city to a standstill with men, women and children lying in drunken stupors practically everywhere (a bit like the West End on New Year's Eve).

By the Way
This is how the term 'mother's ruin' came to be used as a term for strong drink.

Just to show how bad the gin habit had become, the average consumption (including that by kids) in 1730 was over two pints a week. Gin mania was only ended when such soaring duties were loaded on the spirit that it was priced right out of existence. During the 'hangover' period there was rioting in the streets from the slightly wobbly and deeply deprived imbibers.

By the Way
The saddened mob held a funeral procession for 'Madame Geneva' while continuing to drink their favourite tipple under various *noms de plume* like 'Ladies' Delight', 'Cuckold's Comfort' or 'King Theodore of Corsica'. Anyone who informed on them was promptly murdered.

Mugging and Murder
You took your life in your hands if you had to travel around the city, especially at night (London's now like Never-Never Land in comparison). As one reporter put it in 1730: *violence*

and plunder are no longer confined to the highways - the streets of the city are now places of danger; men are knocked down and robbed, nay, sometimes murdered in their own doors, and in the passing from house to house, or from shop to shop. Stagecoaches were being openly held up in Pall Mall, Soho and all the streets leading to and from the city. Even the Lord Mayor himself was jumped and robbed in Chiswick in 1776, in front of his own entourage.

Oddly, the worst of the villains became popular heroes amongst the city folk and more often than not they were cheered as they went daily and sometimes gaily to the gallows, smartly attired in their Sunday best, and stopping for drinks along the way.

Famous Londoners No. 12: *James Maclean*

A resident of posh St James's, he told everyone (particularly ladies) he was an Irish squire and robbed his victims 'with the greatest good breeding'. He reportedly went happily to be hanged, wearing a lace-trimmed silk waistcoat and yellow slippers in finest Moroccan leather (there's no mention of trousers, but we'll take them as read).

Famous Londoners No. 13: *Jack Shepherd*

Hero of the Penny Dreadfuls, highwayman Jack became famous for the number of times he managed to escape from the toughest prisons. He apparently had to get out to satisfy (in all respects) his longtime girlfriend Edgeworth Bess who often helped with his escapes. His most famous away-days were from the deepest dungeon in Newgate, where he'd been chained to the floor, and another from the third floor of an

eighteen-metres-high tower - again chained, but this time handcuffed and manacled as well. He became so infamous that the King's personal portrait painter did one of him too. After being hanged in front of an affectionate, cheering throng of people in 1724, he was found to be carrying a little knife, obviously intended for yet another escape attempt.

Famous Londoners No. 14: *Jonathan Wild*

One of the most notorious criminals of all time. Wild became known as the 'Thieftaker-General of Great Britain and Ireland', as he would round up known thieves, using his own gang. He'd also find stolen goods (which he'd stolen) and return them to the general public, for a fat fee. Outwardly he always appeared to be highly respectable (even though he'd once been a brothel-keeper).

★ WORTH A VISIT? ★

Wild's grand house was situated appropriately at Old Bailey. In fact if you pace fifty-five metres from the corner of Ludgate Hill you get to 30 Old Bailey where his house once stood. It's now a café.

The joke was that most of the stuff Wild offered back, had been stolen by his own gang in the first place. Worse than

HOW DELIGHTFUL - JUST LIKE THE ONE I USED TO HAVE

all that, he sent sixty of these thieving mates to their deaths, collecting a fee for their arrest and prosecution, which annoyed them no end. Eventually the whole scam was detected and Wild was taken to be hanged himself, having been pelted and spat on by the public all the way. Nobody loves a grass. Wild was hanged on a rope made of his own fine lace shirts.

The 'Jonathan Wild Act' made it a crime to make money by returning goods to their owner without arresting or at least splitting on the thief.

By the Way

Mr Wild kept six mistresses at a time in fine style. His 'Lost Property Office', as he called it, earnt him £10,000, and the thief-catching sideline made him a further £2,400. If you deduct the cash paid to all those to whom he had to bung bribes, he still must have come out of it with a cool, tax-free £500,000 in today's money.

★ WORTH A VISIT? ★

This is a real snip. If you want to see Wild's actual skeleton (along with those of a 7 foot, 8 inch giant and a 20 inch midget), go along to the Royal College of Surgeons at 33-35 Lincolns Inn Fields and ask the attendant if he'll let you look round the little museum. It's not usually open to the public but if you ask very nicely it's possible to go in.

Well Hung in the Eighteenth Century

It really wasn't that difficult, if you fancied having your neck stretched, to find a way to get hanged. Simply thieving food was the quickest way, but there were over 150 other offences that carried the death penalty. There seemed to be hardly any difference between the small time thief and the guy, for instance, who cut a woman open in Hyde Park because she swallowed her wedding ring that he'd been after.

A Walk in The Park?

In the 1750s highwaymen rode openly in Hyde Park, tying their horses to the railings and sallying forth to rob anything that moved. In the now highly demure Kensington Gardens, a bell was rung every night to warn all the homeward-bound promenaders and party-goers to gather together in big groups in order to foil the bandits. Stick that in your pipe, all you who claim that London's getting more dangerous!

Let There Be Light

Probably the greatest asset for your average mugger or burglar was darkness, and there was now a real attempt to improve the almost non-existent street lighting. Another helpful move was the replacement of 'Mr Fielding's People' (a tiny private police force) by the famous Bow Street Runners (named because they operated from Bow Street Magistrates' Court, which is still there). These chaps were paid a guinea a week and a divvy of any cash from successful prosecutions.

By the Way

Henry Fielding was the guy who wrote that really rather rude period novel *Tom Jones*, and it was he and his brother (blind) John who commissioned the first six plain-clothed 'thief-takers'. Unfortunately these guys often took the law into their own hands and on one occasion imprisoned twenty-six murder suspects in the St Martin's Round House with all the doors and windows tightly closed. In the morning four were dead. Two died a little later, and the rest were near death from the effects of suffocation.

Fanny Hill

Talking of old classic porn, *Fanny Hill* was written by John Cleland in 1750 for a printer to bail him out of Newgate. John Cleland only got twenty guineas, while the printer made a cool ten grand.

Executions Galore

Although Fielding and his brother thought public executions a touch barbaric, the general public and also, rather strangely, most of the accused, thought otherwise. They had become so commonplace and were so popular, that they were said to have became nothing to the poor 'but an awry neck and a wet pair of breeches'. (Mine would have been more than just wet!) The rich seemed to love a good execution and would pay a fortune for ringside seats. If a wealthy man was being executed, he could forgo the normal old cart that they usually used for the 'delivery' and use his own six horse-drawn landau.

EXCUSE ME! DO YOU MIND?

Hang 'em All

Hangmen were generally hated for good reason. Apart from doing such a horrid job, they would auction their victims' legs and clothes – a sort of grisly perk. They were often drunk or incompetent (or both) and it was not unusual for the poor victim's rellies to hang on their loved one's body to speed up the bitter end.

It was also not unusual to see groups of surgeons fighting for the ten bodies a year allowed for dissection.

. . . And Women

Women had another treat in store. After being hanged the law required that their bodies were to be publicly burned. Some weren't even properly dead when they got to the second bit, which must have been a trifle uncomfortable.

By the Way.

The last woman to get this treatment – which, I might add, was hugely popular with the London crowds – was a certain Margaret Sullivan who was executed in 1788 for merely painting copper coins silver.

By Another Way

Killing illegitimate children was a common crime amongst the poor, accounting for ten per cent of the women strung up at Tyburn. Those nippers that weren't murdered were often left by the roadside (a very common sight) in the hope that someone would pick them up.

★ WORTH A VISIT? ★

Should you happen to be in the Macdonald's at Marble Arch, you will be sitting in the equivalent of the back row at the executions at Tyburn. If that doesn't put you off your burger, nothing will. More ketchup please!

Prisons

Eighteenth-century prisons (there were eighteen in London) were no better than they had ever been and in some cases worse. The debtors' prisons were OK in a funny sort of way, as the inmates were merely kept under lock and key. It was not so much as punishment, but more as a means of making sure he, or his family, repaid what he owed. Visitors could come and go as they pleased and some of these places were described as quite jolly, run by the prisoners themselves while the heavily bribed gaolers looked the other way. As one prison inspector John Howard remarked:

'The prisoners play in the courtyard at skittles, Mississippi, fives, tennis etc,' and went on, 'On Monday night there was a wine club; on Thursday night a beer club; each lasting till one or two in the morning. I need not say how much riot these occasions, and how the sober prisoners, and those that are sick, are annoyed by them.' (Spoilsports.)

PLEASE DON'T NICK THE GLASSES

But London's gaols were not all like this. Most were filthy, crowded and horribly brutal; a breeding ground for the rampant gaol fever. And the government and the City Corporation seemed blind to what was going on. The Clerkenwell Bridewell or, later, the House of Detention (demolished in 1846), was described as a 'great brothel' (and I don't think that means 'great' as in 'good'), while the Fleet Prison turned into the largest brothel in all London. Not surprising, seeing that not only were 'free' prostitutes allowed to work alongside the prisoners, but so were condemned women who actively tried to get pregnant as a way of cheating the noose.

★ WORTH A VISIT? ★

If you go to Clerkenwell Close EC1, it might interest you to know that, back in the eighteenth century, you'd be there for a very specific reason. It is the site of the old Clerkenwell Bridewell Prison. It's now a little-known museum called the House of Detention and the original cells are still there to be seen - if you like that sort of thing.

By The Way

The famous Marshalsea prison was hired out to a local butcher for a fee of £400. He thought of many ways of making a profit, which included packing up to fifty men at a time in tiny cells, each man paying two shillings and sixpence a week for the privilege of sharing a bed with up to three other men.

All Aboard

Worse than all these land-locked prisons were the rotting hulks of old decommissioned men-of war, that were moored in the wider bit of the Thames, and used to hold prisoners. The overcrowded conditions were apparently indescribable. They were so bad that transportation to Australia (where men would be virtual slaves) was looked on as a soft option.

Police Corruption

Many arrested felons never actually managed to get to the prison cell, as the constable in charge of the temporary lock-up was usually up for a bribe (as were witnesses and those on the jury). Many of the richer murderers simply laughed at the gallows as they always knew they could buy their way out. Until 1792, all the fines imposed went straight into the ever deepening pockets of the Justices of the Peace. One of the great scams of the day was for constables to go out into the streets and give beggars a penny, and then claim the ten pound reward for convicting them. Neat!

LONDON PUTS ON WEIGHT

Hell is a city much like London - a populous and smoky city:
Percy Shelley (1792-1822)

London was now the largest city in Europe, but don't get too excited: a relatively fit person could still stroll from one end to the other in no time at all (these days you'd be dead from carbon monoxide fumes before you got a quarter of the way). England, especially in the cities, wasn't exactly squeaky-clean then and was still a very unhealthy place to live in. OK, they didn't have the discharge from cars but just imagine the filthy smogs caused by the thousands of open fires. If you managed to make forty, you were thought to be doing quite well. In 1750 there were 5,200,000 people in the whole of Britain but, although they were still breeding like rabbits (contraception was unheard of), infant mortality was so heavy that it kept the numbers down.

By the Way

Actually condoms were available but were only used by men to avoid catching diseases from their wicked away-matches.

Time for George?

George I had arrived in Britain from Hanover, Germany, in 1714, aged 54, with his two favourite German mistresses. One was thin (nicknamed 'the Maypole'), and one fat ('the Elephant and Castle'). They were to become renowned for their spectacular ugliness. (Could they have been the origin of

Cinderella's ugly sisters?) George had already divorced his wife and, rather sensibly I feel, had her banged up in a German castle on the pretext that she'd been up to no good with a no-good Count called Graf von Kônigsmark.

The British, and particularly Londoners, hated George and his companions from the word go. Throughout history they'd put up with Italian, Scandinavian, Norman, Dutch, Scottish, Welsh and even French rulers, but a non-English-speaking German – and a fat non-English-speaking German come to that – it was all too much. *Nein* thank you!

Apart from being gross, ugly and German, George was quite an oddball; sleeping, receiving visitors and taking all his meals (sauerkraut no doubt) in the same room, guarded by his two 'Pages of the Backstairs', swarthy Turks called Mahomet and Mustapha.

In 1727, poor George suffered a severe attack of diarrhoea (mustaphapoo) which left his face distorted (not surprised) and his right arm hanging limp. He died the following day.

Another George

In 1727 George II, whose father had hated him with gusto, came to the throne. He was described as short and cocky with a passion for fighting (he was the last British king to get personally stuck into battles). Neither his nor his father's contribution to London life had been up to much (sort of understandable as they both preferred Hanover) but, despite this, they were responsible for Kensington Palace, the Broad Walk, the Round Pond and the Serpentine which had been filled by blocking the tiny little Westbourne River. Up to this time, you'd have taken your life in your hands had you ventured into Hyde Park, and it must be said that the Georges at least made it a bit more user-friendly.

By the Way

Poor George died in another embarrassing toilet-related manner. While on the Royal 'Close-Stool' in the morning, his valet heard a noise 'louder than the royal wind', followed by a groan. The King had fallen off the lav, hit his head and died.

And Another George

This one, the third, crowned in 1760, turned out to be worse than his granddad or great-granddad put together, for he liked the idea of running the country without any help from Parliament. This, coupled with his suffering from a rare blood disorder, gave him all the outside appearances of being totally mad.

He was the first English-born, English-speaking Hanoverian King and unfortunately fell madly in love with a pretty fifteen-year-old called Lady Sarah Lennox. He used to see her while she was haymaking on the lawns of Holland House (Holland Park W11) when he was out riding. Unfortunately he, in order to keep the court Germanic, was forced to marry the non-English-speaking, not-nearly-as-pretty, German, Charlotte of Mecklenburg-Strelitz, and even more unfortunately than that, Sarah (the girl he really fancied) was one of the bridesmaids. I bet that cheered him up big time!

CHARMED TO MEET YOU, MY LADY

WHAT?

London Goes Georgian

Georgian architecture became all the rage and the new style was popping up everywhere. The principal designer was William Kent, followed by the famous Robert Adam, who was to become the main architect for the second half of the eighteenth century. Adam, with his brothers (the Adams Family?) built most of the West End and a lot of the great central Squares like St James's, Portman and Fitzroy.

Read All About It!

As more and more people were able to read and write, the need for things for them to read rose spectacularly. Publishers began to make serious loot, but many found producing newspapers, as opposed to books, a bit of a trial. The printers of these broadsheets and news pamphlets teetered between publishing and prison, purely because of the ever-changing laws declaring what could and couldn't be written about. Way back in 1663, a printer in Cloth Street had been pounced on and executed 'in a most foule manner' for urging people to take the law into their own hands if they didn't agree with a particular judgement. Things weren't much better fifty years later.

Life became easier when the Act licensing newspapers was abandoned in 1702 and the first little news-sheet, the *Daily Courant*, with a circulation of 800, was sold out of Elizabeth Mallet's bookshop in Ludgate Hill. The paper was owned by a cartel of twenty booksellers, as were most of the others that were to appear in the first quarter of the century. Writing social tittle-tattle became much easier but editors had to be very careful not to say a word against the Government or Monarch. MP John Wilkes's news-sheet, *North Briton*, broke the rules, as it was said to be openly against George III. Wilkes was thrown into the Tower but he escaped to France, returning some time later to be the hero of all those who hated the King.

★ Worth a Visit? ★

A new statue of the cross-eyed womaniser Wilkes has been erected in Fetter Lane, just off Fleet Street.

Tittle-Tatler

Papers like the highly political *Tatler* in 1709, and later the non-political *Spectator* in 1711 (both now the other way round), appeared in the form of an open letter on current affairs. These were followed by many more before the Stamp Act in 1712 practically closed them down.

Proper papers

By 1760 newspapers were coming and going like women's fashions. One of them, the *Daily Universal Register*, changed its less than snappy name to *The Times* in 1788 and never looked back. Ten years later the *Observer* was born.

Famous Londoners No. 15: *Edmund Curll*

'The unspeakable Curll' was called the 'father of English pornography' and got into big trouble in 1719 with his book *A Treatise in the use of Flogging in Venereal Affairs*. Curll defended himself by saying that, instead of publishing the book to titillate and excite, it was meant as a warning (oh yeah!) on the dangers of flagellation for kicks (some guy had been whipped to death in a Fleet Street brothel that very week). Two other books he published were called *Venus in the Cloister or the Nun in her Smock*, which described in lurid detail the after-dark antics of two nuns, and *The Pleasures of Coition* (look it up). His own book was charmingly entitled *The Case of Seduction . . . the late proceedings at Paris against the Rev. Abbé des Rues for committing Rapes upon 133 Virgins*. He escaped being put in the stocks and pelted with rotten vegetables by distributing a pamphlet to the crowd claiming his innocence.

Famous Londoners No. 16: *Casanova*

Not many people know that Casanova, the most prolific lover in the world, though not actually a Londoner, lived in the city for a while. He came here with £12,000 which he wanted to invest in a lottery - all the rage in France from where he'd just come.

He quickly set up a harem with five German sisters in his Pall Mall lodgings, but found them a bit expensive to keep and moved to Greek Street, Soho. His main prey was the world-famous and beautiful society whore, Kitty Fisher, who had once, apparently, scornfully put the Duke of York's fifty pound note between two bits of bread and eaten it (her fee was £100).

EARLY SANDWICH

By the Way

Oddly enough, the very first sandwich was credited to John Montagu, the Earl of Sandwich in 1762, which he created during a twenty-four-hour card game in London. I wonder if Kitty beat him to it.

Casanova apparently only knew three chat-up words in English – 'I love you!' –which, apparently, had so far stood him in good stead. But young Kitty roared with laughter when she heard him, which totally threw the poor chap. She said, as a concession, he could have her for ten guineas (a real bargain) but he said he could never make love with a woman who couldn't understand him. No comment!

Famous Londoners No. 17: *Alexander Keith*

At 38a Curzon Street, in the middle of the eighteenth century, was the May Fair Chapel, where the 'Rev' Alexander Keith and his four sidekicks married 7,000 couples without so much as a single credential or licence. He became all the rage with bigamists who didn't have to give their real names. The Church became very cross and in 1742 Keith was defrocked and imprisoned for the 'contempt of the Holy and Mother Church'. While he was in prison his assistants carried on a few yards from the original premises. He was responsible for the first proper Marriage Act of 1754 which outlawed unlicensed weddings and instituted the calling of the bans three times. That's the bit where the vicar asks if anyone has any reason why the marriage shouldn't take place.

Famous Londoners No. 18: *James Graham*

As Nell Gwynne's next door neighbour in Pall Mall (albeit nearly a hundred years later) lived the superb Dr James Graham. He became famous in Georgian London for his Temple of Health and Hymen. It boasted not only a scary sounding 'medico-Electrical Apparatus' but a 'grand celestial bed' which rested on forty pillars of twinkly glass and was covered by a mirror-lined dome (wow!). For a considerable amount of cash, couples who'd been having trouble in the - er - baby-making department, could rent the bed and, with the addition of gentle music (probably a string quartet playing in the other room) would be 'guaranteed an heir'. Together with one of his assistants, 'little Emma' (later the infamous famous Lady Hamilton), Dr Graham would show the punters the therapeutic qualities of deep, gooey mud baths - both wearing their elaborate heavily-coiffed wigs, and nothing else.

MUD, MUD-GLORIOUS MUD

Greedy Graham made a fortune from a whole range of hugely expensive elixirs with names like 'Imperial Pills', 'Electrical Aether' and 'Nervous Aethereal Balsam', but all that money was to do him no good, for the poor Doc caught a severe attack of religion in 1787 and ended up, seven years later, barking mad in a lunatic asylum.

★ WORTH A VISIT? ★

Talking of Lady Hamilton, she had a strong connection with the historical but hardly known River Wandle. The best place to find it is in the centre of the Wandsworth one-way system. This little river runs all the way from Croydon (a damn good place to run from) and hits the Thames at Wandsworth Bridge. Admiral Nelson used to fish in the Wandle when staying with Lady Hamilton (it ran through her back garden). She called it 'The Nile' in his honour, because that was where he won one of his most famous battles.

Famous Londoners No. 19: *Mary Tofts*

In December 1726 an extraordinary medical investigation came to an end. Mary Tofts had arrived at Leicester Fields (now Leicester Square) claiming that she'd just given birth to fifteen - wait for it - rabbits!   She said that her whole

HOW D'YOU LIKE RABBITS - MRS TOFTS

reproductive system had been thrown off balance when a rabbit had startled her when she was out walking (good job it wasn't a hedgehog, I say). Her friend and local chemist, John Howard, said he had felt the bunnies leaping about inside her and had even delivered the front half of a four month old skinless rabbit (yukk!!). The medical profession were all taken in at first, particularly a Mr St Andre – Surgeon and Anatomist to His Majesty. Mary then said she was expecting again but, this time, was watched closely and caught redhanded buying her new babies off a back-street second-hand rabbit dealer in Leicester Fields. She was briefly held in prison at the Bridewell accused as a 'vile cheat and imposter', but the charge was dropped and she returned to her husband and three normal children in Godalming, of all places.

Famous Londoners No. 20: *Edward Cross*

The Strand, a rather dull, impersonal street these days, once boasted a bizarre menagerie, just where it crosses with Exeter Street (famous for toyshops). Exeter Change, as the building was called, housed a dealer in wild and exotic animals and birds who, in 1773 sold out to Edward Cross who displayed the beasts along with the most horrible human freaks.

By the Way

In 1826, shortly before it closed, a massive five-ton bull elephant called Chunee suddenly had enough, went mad, and threatened to break out of the menagerie. A civilian firing squad couldn't kill him, so they called for the military who also had no luck after firing a hundred rounds at it (bad shots?). They then sent for a cannon (crikey!) but before it got there the owner managed to finish the poor thing off with a harpoon. The beast was then dissected by ten surgeons, while observed by medical students.

EIGHTEENTH-CENTURY FUN

London, that great cesspool into which all the loungers of the Empire are irresistibly drained: Sir Arthur Conan Doyle

Life in the eighteenth century could well have been more fun than in any other of London's history – providing you had the necessary dosh and especially if you were a man.

Coffee Houses

Would you believe me if I told you that there was once a period when a drink as boring as coffee could have been a real big deal? Or even weirder, that the places where it was drunk could be regarded as being trendy as any new bar or club today?

Coffee in the eighteenth century was a real novelty, as it had only reached these shores in 1662, even though it had been around in Arab countries for donkey's years. It had been discovered by a lowly Arab shepherd boy in Aden, who'd noticed his precious little bleaters wide awake and refusing to go to bed at night. They'd been chewing the red berries off a local bush (*Coffea arabica*).

The newfangled coffee houses (which also served tea and chocolate) became the morning meeting places of anyone who was anyone in the City, and it was in these crowded, smoky places (clay pipes not ciggies) that all major business was discussed. Institutions like Lloyd's, the mammoth marine insurance market, grew from Edward Lloyd's Coffee House in Tower Street, while the Stock Exchange eventually developed from deals made in Jonathan's Coffee House. Francis White's Chocolate House was where all the professional gamblers would rendezvous and that eventually turned into White's, perhaps the most famous and illustrious of all London's gentlemen's clubs. The first White's was destroyed in 1733 when a fire broke out in one of the gaming-rooms called, rather appropriately, 'Hell'. At the peak of their popularity there were 500 coffee houses.

WHICH FIRST?

Bleed You Sir?

At the now rather posh Cheyne Walk there used to be an institution run by a Spanish barber named Don Saltero, an ex-servant of Sir Hans Sloane, the super-rich Chelsea doctor (of Sloane Square fame). Saltero was quite a lad by all accounts. While you were sipping your coffee, Saltero could shave you, cut your hair, bleed you (supposed to make one feel much better) or pull a tooth or two. And while doing all this, he would often stop to play the violin or chant verses at you. I wonder if a place like that would work these days? I think I'll stick to pubs, barbers, and doctors.

★ WORTH A VISIT? ★

Next time you're in Covent Garden, stand under the entrance of St Paul's Church and try to imagine Tom King's Coffee House, which was little more than a shed. It was frequented by those gentlemen of early eighteenth-century society who seemed to stay out all night. When King, an Eton scholar, died, his widow – the illustrious Moll King – took over and was constantly in front of the beak for running a disorderly house. The writer Smollett described an evening there: 'Banter and I accompanied Bagwell to Moll King's Coffee House, where, after he had kicked half-a-dozen hungry whores, we left him to sleep on a bench.' Whatever turns you on.

By the Way

William Hogarth's★ dad – an ex-classics teacher – decided to open a coffee house where only Latin could be spoken. As payment for this gross act of over-the-top pretentiousness, he went bust and ended up in debtors' prison. Prisons became a recurring theme of his son's work. (He must've taken his easel on visiting days.)

WANT TO PAINT ME, MATE?

By Another Way

To get things in perspective, as well as coffee houses, there were 207 inns, 447 taverns, 5,875 beer-houses and a staggering 8,659 brandy-shops. They liked their drink in those days.

★ One of our most famous painters.

Pleasure Gardens

If coffee houses were the places to be seen in the mornings, the wealthy man about town (or anyone else come to that) could do far worse than visit one of the 200 pleasure gardens in the evening. The most famous and most imitated of all was Vauxhall, opened just before the Restoration in 1660 and situated on the south side of the river where Westminster Bridge is now (before the bridge was opened in 1750, it could only be reached from the city by boat).

The gardens were free to enter and incredibly beautiful. There were long, winding, leafy walkways between scented bushes and trees, lit by 3,000 lamps. Musicians tinkled and plucked on harp or flute at every clearing. There were stalls and bars selling delicious food and drink, there were acrobats and performing animals and - well you name it. This was how it was described by a scribbler of the time:

> *Now the Summer months come round,*
> *Fun and pleasure will abound,*
> *High and low and great and small,*
> *Run in droves to view Vauxhall.*
> *See the motley crew advance,*
> *Led by Folley in the Dance,*
> *English, Irish, Spanish, Gaul*
> *Drive like mad to dear Vauxhall*
>
> *Each profession, ev'ry trade,*
> *Here enjoy refreshing shade,*
> *Empty is the cobbler's stall,*
> *He's gone with tinker to Vauxhall,*
> *Here they drink, and here they cram,*
> *Chicken, pasty, beef and ham,*
> *Women squeak and men drunk fall.*
> *Sweet enjoyment of Vauxhall.*

By the Way

A huge firework display was held in Green Park in April 1749 to celebrate the end of the war in Scotland. Unfortunately it was more of a display than they bargained for. A stray rocket went off too quickly and lit the other 10,650. One hundred musicians legged it, people threw themselves in the pond, and one poor girl had all her burning clothes ripped off.

Dark Secrets

The idea of a park only open at night seems rather groovy to me, but, as you can imagine (or maybe you can't), all sorts of other things went on that your more, how shall we say, respectable Londoners were not too happy about. As well as all the illuminated walkways, there were lots of narrow, maze-like darker ones. Now, it really doesn't need me to suggest what happens, if you get a heady combination of darkness, bushes, strong drink, and people of opposite sexes out to have a good time. Whores lurked provocatively in the shadows, and the narrow lanes became like a spider's web for any poor unfortunate damsel (or bloke come to that) who inadvertently sauntered off the main path. The park became of great concern to the owners and visitors alike.

FANCY SOME FUN, MY LORD?

Later in the 1730s supper-boxes, statues, music rooms and Chinese pavilions were added, and an entrance fee of one shilling* (£3.75), was charged, intended to keep the riff-raff at bay. In 1764 the infamous dark walkways were fenced off, but were soon broken down by hooligans.

*This went up to 2s (£7.50) in 1792, and 4s 6d (£16.88) in 1821.

Despite all this, the Vauxhall Gardens prospered and became the centre for London's society – with grand concerts, firework displays, fancy dress parties and even replays of famous battles that we, the English, had once won. The gardens closed in 1840 (after an astonishing 180 years) when the owners went bankrupt – and more's the pity I say.

★ WORTH A VISIT? ★

If you want to walk in exactly the same location as the pleasure gardens, they're marked by Goding Street to the west, St Oswald's Place to the east, Leopold Street and Vauxhall Walk to the north, and Kennington Lane to the south.

By the Way

At the infamous Spring Gardens at Charing Cross there used to be a famous sundial with a 'jet d'eau'. If a person, on inspecting the dial, stepped on a particular stone, he or she

would be soaked by a jet of water. This was thought to be hilarious at the time. Hmmm!

The English Grotto

As an example of one of the hundreds of smaller pleasure gardens, I'll mention the English Grotto at Roseman Street, Clerkenwell. In 1769 it was advertised thus: 'a Grand Grotto Garden and Gold and Silver Fish Repository'. It had a fountain, a deep grotto (hugely popular in those days), a water mill which created a rainbow, and presumably, tons of goldfish. Admission: 6d.

Sadler's Wells

Sadler's Wells theatre was called such because it was started by a guy named Sadler who had built it in 1683 to cash in on the medicinal well (mineral water) that was on his property. There were lots of these spas at the time. This one attracted up to 500 people a day and the theatre pulled in an audience made up of 'strolling damsels, half-pay officers, peripatetic [travelling] tradesmen, tars [sailors] butchers and others that are musically inclined.' (Musically inclined butchers? I think not.) As well as all the standard acts, it included the famous resident clown, Grimaldi.

★ Worth a Visit? ★

It seems pretty unlikely now but at the beginning of the eighteenth century, Streatham Common was the home of one of the most famous spas in Britain. Its waters had been discovered by a ploughman in 1659 who, not put off by its 'mawkish taste', found it to be good for worms (I presume that means good for getting rid of worms) and for the eyes. Concerts were held at the spa and it became one of the smartest places to be seen out walking in the evening (these days you take your life in your hands). People from every walk of life fell over each other to buy Streatham Spa water fresh each morning at St Paul's Church Yard, Temple Bar and the Royal Exchange. Streatham Spa closed in 1792. Presumably the water's still lurking there, waiting for some entrepreneur to discover it again

Tea time

Did you know that at the end of the Tottenham Court Road (now ninety per cent hi-fi and computer shops) near Warren Street tube station, there used to be the Adam and Eve Tea Gardens? This was a large peaceful garden featuring long, shady arbours for tea-drinking, and skittle alleys (ever so popular in those days) for the more energetic. By the end of the eighteenth century, sad to say, it was completely hemmed in by buildings and became simply a haunt for thieves and prostitutes.

By the Way

Tea was regarded as the ultimate of luxuries with huge curative powers. At the beginning of the eighteenth century it cost £10 a pound (an unbelievable £650 in today's money). As you might imagine, all early tea caddies were locked. What would they have made of triangular tea bags?

Fairs

If your meagre wages wouldn't run to pleasure gardens, then there was all the fun of the free fairs all around the city. On the north side was the fascinating Smithfield or Bartholomew's Fair, which was reasonably respectable with conjurors, boxers, rope-dancers, fortune-tellers and even the odd theatrical production. On the south side, however, was Southwark Fair, which, being Southwark, was a very different kettle of all sorts of things.

It was originally on just for three days in September, but rapidly grew to two weeks (some went on for six), becoming known as Our Lady's Fair. It was held throughout all the grimy little streets in Southwark, and was famous for such turns as 'Mr Fawkes with his Amazing and Curious Indian Birds', 'James Figg, Prizefighter and Swordsman', the 'Lee and Harper Acting Booth', 'Miller the German Giant' and 'Cadman the Slack-Rope Performer'. Then there were performing monkeys, waxwork shows (dead popular in those pre-photo or telly days) and exhibitions of the wildest animals and the worstest freaks imaginable. In those days gross physical deformity was seen as a positive bonus if you were poor and needed to scratch a living.

By the Way

One of the most famous waxworks of the time was that of the Countess of Heningburgh lying in state with her 365 children - all born in one go. Blimey, that's a lot of wax, let alone children!

By 1763 Southwark Fair was finally closed down, as it also had become simply a hunting ground for pick-pockets and prostitutes. The 'May Fair' held in the Shepherd's Market area during the first two weeks of May, was almost as bad and was described as the 'chiefest nursery of evil' because of the offence it was causing the residents, who were gradually becoming posher and posher.

★ WORTH A VISIT? ★

Shepherd's Market, Mayfair, is still London's most notorious area for up-market ladies of the night (so I'm told!!).

Famous Londoners No. 21: *James Boswell*

Boswell, the famous diarist, was a real playboy at night. 'Talking of prostitutes,' he wrote, 'I am surrounded with numbers of free-hearted ladies of all kinds: from the splendid madam at fifty guineas a night, down to the civil nymph with white-thread stockings who tramps along the Strand and will resign her engaging person to your honour for a pint of wine and a shilling.' Apparently the girls in Hyde Park only cost him sixpence!

Famous Londoners Nos. 22 and 23: *Charlotte Hayes and Dennis O'Kelly*

Two houses, 91 and 92 (just next to Half Moon Street) in Piccadilly became the rather inappropriately named Cloisters, maybe London and Mayfair's most notorious brothel. It was run by Charlotte Hayes and her hubby 'Colonel' Dennis O'Kelly who'd met in Fleet prison. They were released, due to an amnesty for all prisoners when George III came to the throne, and raised the money through their up-market connections.

Although the Cloisters catered for both men and women of all ages, charging an outlandish fifty guineas a night, it became most famous for a remarkable parrot which, despite every kind of distraction (if you know what I mean!), could sing and whistle the 104th Psalm.

While Charlotte ran the business, O'Kelly was away at the races. Despite being severely rich and owning a world-beating horse called Eclipse (eighteen races and never beaten), he was never allowed to join the dead posh jockey club.

Famous Londoners No. 24: *Samuel Johnson*

The eighteenth century was very much a man's world and, apart from their coffee houses, men liked evening clubs that allowed them to rub shoulders with those of similar interests. One of the most famous clubmen of the time, and a passionate Londoner, was Doctor Samuel Johnson. He is probably the most well-known author outside Shakespeare – not necessarily for his books, but his witty quips and acid piss-taking. He hung out at 'The Club' at the Turk's Head (now gone) in Gerrard Street, in the heart of Soho. He founded the club with James Boswell (as previously mentioned), another well-known 'clever dick' who was to write his mate, Johnson's, biography. It was Johnson who came out with the famous and often quoted one-liner: 'When a man is tired of London, he is tired of life; for there is in London all that life can afford', a sentiment that holds true for me to this day. Despite his enormous fame, the poor doc was often so poor that he feared that even the milkman might arrest him for debt.

★ WORTH A VISIT? ★

There are two statues of the old doc, one in St Paul's and one at the other end of Fleet Street, neither of which shows his badly pockmarked face (marked from 'the king's-evil', a nasty little disease of the time).

Famous Londoners No. 25: *Philip Astley*

The first circus to be seen in Britain was started by Philip Astley, 'a man with the proportions of Hercules and the voice of a senator'. He erected a temporary structure in the Westminster Bridge Road in 1770 'for the exhibition of equestrian skill'. The fact that he only had one horse (given as a leaving-present by the cavalry) and no licence, didn't seem to matter.

By 1780 his temporary, canvas-covered ring was replaced by a proper building, renamed Astley's Amphitheatre and it presented visiting clowns (including Grimaldi), acrobats and magicians as well as herds of horses. Charles Dickens loved the place and it survived three major fires until being pulled down in 1893.

Baiting and Fighting

There used to be this place called Hockley in the Hole just off today's Farringdon Road EC1, that took over as the centre for all animal baiting when those places in Southwark started to lose their audiences. Dangerous places these, for at one of them the actual owner was eaten by his own bear (served him right) and the advertisement for another read:

One of the largest and most mischievous bears that was ever seen in England to be baited to death, with the other variety of bull and bear baiting, as also a wild bull to be turned loose in the game place with fireworks all over him. To begin exactly at three o'clock in the afternoon, because the sport continues long.

Men at Hockley also fought with swords and daggers, but these fights were stage-managed carefully to avoid serious injury. At Figg's Amphitheatre in, would you believe, Oxford Street, prizefighters would battle it out bare-knuckled and the contests were announced in all the public prints (forerunners of newspapers). Such giants as Jack Broughton and Mendoza the Jew were locked together in battles that went on for as long as sixty rounds, and there were women's contests featuring the champion of champions, the Massive Martha Jones, a Billingsgate fishwife who sounds just the sort of girl you'd want to take home to meet your mother.

Bethlehem

If you were looking for something amusing and a little different to do with the family on a wet Sunday afternoon in the 1700s, you could do far worse than take a trip up to Bethlehem Royal Hospital or Bedlam (where the Imperial

War Museum is now), a huge and well-known lunatic asylum. On arrival you would enter the vast entrance hall to be confronted by Cibber's huge statue of two loonies, *Madness and Melancholy*, reputedly modelled on two of the inmates. From there you would progress to the main gallery where all the most seriously disturbed

LOOK, MAMA! THERE'S A GREAT ONE — HERE.

residents would be chained to the walls, or in barred cells, for you to gawp and laugh at.

Any inmates that got a little out of hand would be whipped like animals. In 1770 the authorities noticed that the inmates seemed not to like this treatment that much, but they didn't stop it as they were making so much dosh in contributions. Instead they decided to make it a ticket-only affair. Oh boy, and we complain about the way our mental patients are treated these days!

British Museum

If watching wackos wasn't quite your scene, you could always pop along to the newly-opened (1759) British Museum. This fine establishment is located in Bloomsbury which was then on the outskirts of London - now it's in the middle. Actually, having said that, you probably couldn't just pop along, because a) they only allowed ten visitors at a time, b) it was only open for three hours a day and c) would only admit those who'd applied in writing and were approved by the librarian.

The museum kicked off with, amongst others, the aforementioned Sir Hans Sloane's collection of antiquities, bought for £20,000 - far less than half its real value.

By the Way

The £300,000 necessary to start and house the museum project in Great Russell Street was raised by one of the first public lotteries.

By Another Way.

If you had looked out of the back windows of the British Museum, you'd have looked upon farm land as far as the eye could see. These days the first farm land would start somewhere beyond Watford.

Shopping

St James's Street, rather like it is today, had shops mostly for the better off man-about-town, from hatters to shoemakers to tailors, to gunsmiths and winesuppliers. Visit Jermyn Street, where all the wigmakers, shirtmakers, tobacconists, snuff dealers and barbers used to be, and you'll have an almost uncanny and not unpleasant feeling of years gone by. Then stroll up any of the lanes that run into Piccadilly and drop into

Fortnum and Mason's, the exotic food emporium started in 1770 by Charles Fortnum (ex-footman to George III) and his mate, John Mason. Fortnum and Mason began by selling second-hand half-used candles from the Palace. Fortnum's job had been to fill the royal candelabras, so candles were a perk of the job.

Hatchards the bookshop is still only a couple of doors away from where it started in Piccadilly in 1797. Smart women went to Covent Garden or the Strand for their fashionable clothes which were all put together, as they still are to this day, in the dingy sweat shops of the East End.

REGENCY LONDON

Parks are the lungs of London: William Windham 1808

B_y 1811 it had become more and more obvious that old King George III was now as mad as you could get, and would never be able to carry out his official duties again. It was time for his son, the hugely unpopular playboy and society dilettante George, Prince of Wales, to take over as Prince Regent. He was so unpopular that he was hissed, stoned and spat at as he drove to open Parliament in 1817.

George ruled as Prince Regent until 1820 when he became George IV on the death of his father. This period of history became known as the Regency: a term which covers the fashion taste, style and morals of an extraordinary era.

One would have been forgiven for thinking that, to look at, the young Prince Regent was outrageously gay, even by today's standards, and especially in contrast to his stuffy old dad, 'Farmer' George. The lad was at the same time, foppish, outrageous, extravagant and an out-and-out player (in 1787 he overspent by £80,000). But there was nothing 'funny' about our George when it came to his sexual preferences. He'd had a mistress, the much older, beautiful but married actress, Mary Robinson, since his teens, and later, the twice-widowed, twenty-nine-year-old Mrs Fitzherbert, whom he eventually married secretly and illegally. A curate was especially released from the Fleet debtors' prison, on the promise of £500, to conduct the ceremony behind locked doors.

By the Way

George's choice of a proper wife had been less fortunate. Princess Caroline of Brunswick was seldom known to change her underwear and consequently stank to high heaven. On top of that she cursed and swore, was sexually promiscuous (she even spent the night with the first mate of the boat bringing her to England) and was generally thought to be round the bend. The Prince could only get through the marriage ceremony and the wedding night (they only did it the once) by getting completely drunk. From then on they only communicated by letter.

Famous Londoners No. 26: *John Nash*

The young king employed the man of the moment, stylewise, John Nash to do up his homes; the almost obscenely opulent Carlton House, and the way over-the-top (but fab) Royal Pavilion at Brighton (still there) which looks like a cross between a Sultan's temple and an Indian restaurant.

Nash, a snub-nosed, dwarf-like genius, became the King's friend (he was almost as flashy) and, with seemingly limitless funds, became responsible for much of the way the stylish part of London looks today: flamboyant but graceful, with sweeping crescents and Italian-style terraces surrounding glorious parks like Regent's and Marylebone. Bestest of all was the staggeringly beautiful, curved Regent Street whose construction involved the demolition of 700 small shops (and which has been so sadly abused and ravaged in later years).

> *Augustus at Rome was for building renowned*
> *And of marble he left what for brick he had found:*
> *But is not our Nash, too, not a master*
> *He found London brick and he leaves it all plaster.*

Later, areas like St John's Wood, Belsize Park and that whole bit going up to Hampstead, were to echo Nash's magnificent style.

By the Way

George IV, after having bamboozled his parliament into paying for thirty years of splendiferous embellishment to Carlton House, ordered its destruction, and then persuaded Parliament to shell out for refurbishing that rather ugly building, Buckingham Palace, in 1825.

★ WORTH A VISIT? ★

If you're walking along the Victoria Embankment, by the Thames, you'll come across Cleopatra's Needle. This eighteen-metres-high obelisk was cut out of the Aswan quarries in ancient Egypt (1475 BC) and is decorated with carvings of the various gods and symbols representing Pharaoh Tethmosis III. It had been lying neglected in the sand at Alexandria before Mohammed Ali (no, not that one!) gave it to the British in 1819. Buried underneath it are many artefacts of British life, including twelve pictures of what were regarded as the most beautiful Englishwomen of the day, presumably for future generations to laugh at. I wonder who got the job of choosing.

Police-Free

Although the main highways out of town were dangerous, the aristocracy still saw little need for a police force and a bill to authorise a single police authority was chucked out in 1785. The flamboyant Prince Regent would often walk in public through the streets, seeming to enjoy the attempts to jostle, ridicule and even kiss him.

Famous Londoners No. 27: *Lord Gordon*

Lord George Gordon was the son of Cosmo Gordon, Duke of Gordon, and an eccentric MP from the second half of the eighteenth century. He was famous for getting his elegant knickers in the biggest twist ever over the Catholic Relief Act of 1778 (giving Catholics certain rights of ownership).

His march on the House of Commons in 1780 got completely out of hand and the mob started burning any buildings with any Catholic connections, and then any buildings at all. The looting and burning lasted a fortnight and during that time the mob accounted for the destruction of the Catholic Chapel at Moorfields, Bow Street Magistrates Court, the Bank of England (see *Good Places to Loot*) and prisons like Newgate and the Clink, which were ransacked and the inmates released. Eventually the troops were called in and they had to kill 450 demonstrators and execute 25 others to shut 'em up. Gordon went down for treason and rather appropriately ended up in Newgate where, like anyone with any cash, he spent the rest of his days entertaining his mates in grand style with daily lunches and fortnightly dances.

★ WORTH A VISIT? ★

Borough High Street again. On the eastern side of the street stood the infamous King's Bench Prison which dated back to

LET ME IN!

the early sixteenth century. After being rebuilt, following Gordon and his lads' severe torching, it got a reputation for amazing laxness. It was described in 1828 as 'the most desirable place of incarceration in London'. Its main courtyard thronged with barbers, chandlers, hatters, oyster-sellers, tailors and piano-makers. It had thirty gin shops and a regular cook who would serve the wealthier inmates on a daily basis. The poorer ones took turns begging at the gate.

Famous Londoners No. 28: *Richard Trevithick*

If you'd happened to be walking along the north end of Gower Street WCI on Christmas Eve in 1801 you couldn't have helped but notice a small circular railway track, which Richard Trevithick was using to show off his brand new steam engine which pulled a dear little carriage. If you could have afforded a shilling you would have ridden on the first railway ever. Unfortunately, all concerned saw it more as a fairground stunt and proper railways, as such, were to take another twenty-eight years before they reached London. Travel on the ground, in any way, shape or form, was simply archaic and had hardly improved since medieval times. Balloon flights were quite common, but again, Londoners never imagined that there could be any future in travelling by air.

By the Way

Trevithick went bankrupt in 1811 while trying to earn a crust in Peru. Guess who lent him the money to get home? Robert Stephenson, the man credited as the father of steam travel, whom he'd met by pure chance. Funny that.

★ WORTH A VISIT? ★

Have any of you younger readers heard of the Lowther Arcade? I bet you wish you'd been there. It was a glass-domed arcade running off the Strand (where Coutts Bank is now) and was just a whole series of wonderful toyshops. The better-off kids literally dragged their parents there.

Famous Londoners No. 29: *Thomas Pitt*

Lord Camelford, one of the famous Pitts, was a fabulous eccentric who got his kicks stirring up fights. He was immensely rich having inherited his fortune at the age of eighteen but, instead of living in the family mansion in Park Lane, he chose to live over a shop in Bond Street because it was nice and close to the Prince of Wales Coffee House where he hung out. Often in fancy dress, and always accompanied by a massive black prizefighter, he would take the mickey out of all the dandies as he walked the West End streets (as you can, if you're with a massive black prizefighter). He became famous in 1802 when the whole of London was ordered to light up their windows to celebrate the end of the war with France. Camelford would have none of it and kept his windows shuttered. Eventually a screaming mob outside, inflamed by the Lord himself - brandishing a pistol at the window – turned into a riot that became known as the Siege of Bond Street. The colourful Pitt was eventually killed, aged 29, in a duel following a tiff with a friend whom he'd known to be a brilliant shot.

Famous Londoners No. 30: *Theresa Berkely*

In the 1830s there were twenty places that the well informed pervert-about-town could go to get beaten up in comfort. Typical was Theresa Berkely's establishment at 28 Charlotte Street, where her strict governesses could birch you, whip you with a cat-o'-nine-tails, cudgel you, prick you with needles, half hang you, cut your veins, sting you with nettles, scratch you with holly or gorse – whatever turned you on. The speciality of the house, however, was a special whipping machine called The Berkely Horse

THANK YOU MA'M. THAT WAS DELIGHTFUL

which had a revolving wheel with birch canes attached and a gymnasium horse to which the 'client' was strapped. Sure. beats Alton Towers!

Famous Londoners No. 31: *Arthur Thistlewood*

Farmer's son Arthur hated the way the country was going under George IV, so decided to proclaim a republic. Unfortunately, in order to do this and seize London, he realised he had to murder the entire cabinet who were, luckily for him, planning to have supper together round at Lord Harrowby's house on 23rd February 1820. Unluckily for him, his lack of secrecy led to the government finding out what was afoot. The police surrounded his house in Cato Street (off the Edgware Road) and, during the siege, a police-constable was killed by Thistlewood himself. Poor old Arthur was later hanged at Newgate Gaol.

★ WORTH A VISIT? ★

If you're lucky enough to be dining in the superb Tate Gallery restaurant (the one with the Whistler murals covering the walls) and you feel a slight shiver run down your spine, there's a good reason. You are sitting where the cells of the old Millbank Prison (completed in 1821 and pulled down in 1935) were situated.

Zoo Time

A wacky combination of characters led to the beginning of the Zoological Society of London in Regent's Park in 1828 – Sir Stamford Raffles, who practically invented Singapore, and Sir Humphrey Davy, who gave us the miner's safety lamp. Just think, in a world free of television, cinema, photographs and foreign travel, how live animals from far distant lands must have gobsmacked the public.

In fact, the first appearance of the ridiculous-looking giraffe spawned a fashion for blotchy, look-alike fabrics. As the century progressed, Londoners were treated to a whole series of new animals as they pitched up from far and wide. The first chimp (called Tommy) to arrive in 1835 caused a sensation, and this is what was written by Thomas Hood:

The folks in town are nearly wild
To go and see the monkey child
In gardens of Zoology
Whose proper name is Chimpanzee.
To keep this baby free from hurt
He's dressed in a cap and a Guernsey Shirt; [poor devil]
They've got him a nurse and he sits on her knee
And she calls him her Tommy Chimpanzee

Then they came thick and fast – a pair of bison (particularly thick) in 1847, a hippo in 1850, an orang-utan in 1851, a spooky-looking giant anteater in 1853, sea-lions in 1856 and two massive African elephants in 1867. The first koala bear ever to be seen outside Australia arrived in 1880.

By the Way

When the keeper came to check Alice (one of the new jumbos) on Bank Holiday 1867, the poor old dear had over a foot of her trunk mysteriously missing. Strange but true!

C'MON – WHAT HAVE YOU DONE WITH IT?

The zoo was supplemented in 1834 by many of the animals from the Royal Menageries at Windsor and the Tower of London, and it pioneered the very first reptile, insect, and fish house (aquarium). London Zoo, as it soon became known, was originally set up purely for scientific study, but the powers that be (or were) soon realised that there was big money in them there beasts (30,000 visitors in the first six months) and besides, the damn critters were eating them out of house and home. This first zoo, designed by Decimus Burton, must have been simply fabulous, as the animals were kept in weird and wonderful exotic follies, even though the keepers soon realised that the animals didn't get the joke.

. . . and Another Zoo

It's not very well known, but another massive and much more popular zoo, just east of Vauxhall Pleasure Gardens, called the Surrey (God knows why) Literary, Scientific and Zoological Institution, opened in 1856. It was founded by showman Edward Cross, the guy who had the cramped menagerie on the Strand (remember) and it could hold over 10,000 people. Despite its rather grand title, it was much more of a leisure park (like Chessington), staging massive spectacles like the Battle of Sebastopol which featured many of the animals – bears, elephants, lions and camels.

By the Way

In the Second World War they killed most of the wild animals fearing their escape should London Zoo be bombed. The rest they evacuated to Ireland. They also cut all the snakes' heads off and ate all the fish (very scientific).

ZOO CANTEEN

THAT PLEURONECTES PLATESSA WAS DELICIOUS

Pleasure Beasts

Other establishments soon realised that they had to have animals to keep up, but usually had to go one better. In the Spring Gardens (SW1), you could visit 'Toby the Sapient [wise] Pig' who could, by all accounts, play cards, spell, tell the time and mind-read (blimey, that's cleverer than me). In

Piccadilly, at William Bullock's fantastic Egyptian Exhibition Hall, they had a famous mermaid – half monkey, half fish (shouldn't that be 'mermonkey'?) – a family of Laplanders complete with reindeer, a mammoth's skeleton (dead) and many freak animals and humans, including the world famous sixty centimetre 'General' Tom Thumb.

By the Way

'General' Tom Thumb arrived at the Egyptian Hall in weeny splendour – a tiny carriage with midget coachmen, and pulled by four of the littlest Shetland ponies ever seen.

★ WORTH A VISIT? ★

If you stop for a coffee in the Richoux Café, Piccadilly, you will be at the very site of the Egyptian Hall, which was pulled down in 1905.

VICTORIAN LONDON

*The man who can dominate a London dinner-table can
dominate the world:* Oscar Wilde

In 1837 a miniscule, eighteen-year-old,
grumpy, bug-eyed girl called Victoria
came to the throne, stamped her tiny
foot and said she wanted to live in
Buckingham Palace with her mum, the
Duchess of Kent (albeit at different ends).
It's been the royal residence ever since.
George IV, blessed with the attention
span of a gnat, had obviously got
bored with it and, typically, left the
inside unfinished. Those in the top circles
rather looked down on the poor thing (Buck House - not
Victoria) and regarded it as somewhat 'uncomfortable and
inconvenient'.

But not quite as 'inconvenient' as the disgusting conditions
most of little Vicky's loyal subjects in inner London had to put
up with. In those pre-birth-control-for-all days, the
population had doubled since 1800 and by the time the mini-
queen died it had ballooned to five times. To make matters
worse, each year the population swelled with the thousands of
country poor who, finding themselves unemployed after
haymaking, hit the big city in an effort to find some way of
staying alive.

Housing in the capital was a massive prob (especially if you
didn't have any), and certainly at the beginning of the century
nobody really seemed to do much about the appalling
overcrowding. The actual City, by contrast, was deserted in the

evenings after everyone had gone home from work. The reason was simple: the poor couldn't afford to live there (and still can't) and the rich didn't want to (and still don't).

Other Work

Anyone who had any sort of job in Victorian times was regarded as lucky. Some had to do the most awful things simply to survive, proving the widening gap between the haves and the have-nots. Working conditions for the badly-off in London were as bad as ever, with most shops or offices opening at eight or nine in the morning and not shutting their doors until ten or eleven at night.

Poverty-stricken river fishermen trawled for a precarious living from unlikely places such as Hammersmith★. 'Mudlarks' scoured the Thames's beaches in search of coal spilt out of the barges, or anything that could be sold in the market. Women would sieve mountains of refuse, for rags and bones, while old men and women would collect dogs' muck, called 'pure' (used in the curing of leather), to avoid being thrown in the workhouse. A bucketful a day (that's a load of crap) meant that they could eat and have a roof over their heads (I hope they washed their hands before supper).

The poor kids who also had to work (there was no lower age limit) had no government control on their hours until 1886 when laws were brought in which went some way to protect the under-eighteens.

★ You'd probably die if you ever tried to eat anything out of the river these days.

Little boy sweeps climbed into, and often got stuck in, filthy, lofty chimneys. Others worked in terrible factory conditions for cruel masters. And there were all those forced into begging, thieving or selling their bodies for mere pennies.

Often poor people had to walk many miles to and from where they worked, and that was how the infamous 'rookeries' came about.

Rookeries

There was bad, and there was very bad, and then there were the abominable blocks of rat-infested rooming-houses called 'rookeries' throughout the centre of the city, that grew because people had to be relatively near to where they worked.

In Hanover Square W1 (now dead posh) in 1842, 1,465 familes shared 2,147 festering rooms – and that was typical of hundreds of rookeries. In Church Lane, Westminster, in 1841, 27 dwellings managed to pack in 655 people, some of them even carrying on their trade in the same squashed premises.

This figure rose to 1,095 by 1847. In a letter to *The Times*, a year later, 54 less than thrilled inhabitants wrote:

> We are Sur,
>   as it may be, livin in a Wilderniss, so far as the rest of London knows anything of us, or as the rich and great people care about. We live in muck and filthe. We aint got no privez [lavs]. no dust bins, no drains, no water splies ...We al of us suffer, and the numbers are ill, and iff the Colera comes Lord help us ...

Admittedly it reads a bit like a letter to the *Sun* (0 out of 10 for spelling) but we get the point.

Not Much Better

If the rookeries were the most awful of the places to live, the whole of the East End came a pretty good second. Here's a description of Bethnal Green in the mid-nineteenth century by William Cotton, a banker, philanthropist and well-known jolly good egg:

> ... its courts and alleys are almost countless, and overwhelming with men, women, boys, dogs, cats, pigeons, and birds. Its children are ragged, sharp, weasel-like; brought up from their cradle - which is often an old box or an egg-chest - to hard living and habits of bodily activity. Its men are mainly dock labourers, poor costermongers, poor silk weavers, clinging hopelessly to a withered handicraft, the lowest kind of thieves, with a sprinkling of box and toy makers, shoe makers and cheap cabinet makers. Its women are mostly hawkers, seamstresses, the coarsest order of prostitutes, and aged stall keepers. On Sunday the whole neighbourhood is like a fair.

CHEER UP, MY DEAR.
THIS PLACE WILL BE WORTH
A FORTUNE IN A HUNDRED
AND FIFTY YEARS.

ESTATE AGENT

It's almost funny reading it, when you think that these days, estate agents (God bless them) will tell you that Bethnal Green is regarded as up-and-coming or even the place to be.

Disease Strikes

Back to cholera. You couldn't blame the hard-done-by Londoners for being a teeny bit alarmed. Cholera grabbed the city by the throat in 1849 and over 14,000 people tragically vacated the rookeries and slums for new underground residences in the emergency cemeteries all over the city. Typically of that time, very little was done about it, so cholera was as good as invited back six years later. Actually the only thing they did do to make things better, made things much, much worse.

Previously, doctors had thought that cholera was caused by 'foul vapours' in the air caused by rotting vegetables and excrement. A big deal was made of sluicing down the streets and sending all the garbage etc. into the sewers and so the epidemic was spread more widely and quickly. The connection between cholera and the water supply was not stumbled upon for another twenty years. Apart from its cholera, London was still not the best place you'd choose to be born in, as one in three kids was still dying before the age of one.

Old Man River

One of the main reasons for all this sickness had to be the state of poor Old Father Thames, which had never been worse.

Even as late as 1800, you could've still caught a nice Thames salmon from the banks bang in the middle of town, and in the summer months people could always be seen swimming off Westminster Bridge (until modesty as well as filth got the better of them).

In contrast, by Victorian times a glass of vintage Thames water was said to contain more horrid little organisms than the whole population of the world (according to architect Sidney Smith). Newfangled flushing loos and the increasing network of sewers were all very well, but where did they all run into? You're right – into the poor old river. And where did all the private water companies get their water from? You're right again.

By the Way

The long, stifling summer of 1858 lowered the level of the Thames to such a degree that 'The Great Stink' threatened to close Parliament. There's been many great stinks in Parliament since, but largely self-made.

★ WORTH A VISIT? ★

When walking down the marvellous King's Road in Chelsea (worth a visit in its own right), pause outside No. 120 and reflect that it was once the premises of a certain Thomas Crapper in the 1860s, a plumber and sanitary engineer whose name seems to have gone down in history.

Foreigners Galore

It wasn't all doom and gloom. London, like New York, has always been famous for its immigrant population – it's what gives a city its special fizz. But who were they, and why did they come?

For a start there were 29,000 poor Jews in a Whitechapel ghetto, another 6,000 in St George's Fields, nearly 8,000 in Mile End and another 7,000 in Bethnal Green. The Jewish population had been swollen by the thousands who arrived after escaping the persecution in Poland. They largely replaced the Irish who'd either taken themselves off overseas (particularly America where they all seemed to have become movie stars or cops) or gone to the north-west of London to work on the railways. The Irish community eventually settled in King's Cross, Camden Town, Kentish Town, Holloway, Kilburn and Willesden which is made pretty obvious should you visit any of those areas on a Friday night (especially after the pubs have closed).

Jewish people, because they're usually brilliant at whatever they do, particularly when it comes to business (and because they only looked after their own people), soon became hated by the locals. This is why, when Jack the Ripper (see page 195) was larking about, they were the first to be accused by the mob.

It wasn't long before the Jews began to show all the signs of prosperity and, as they prospered, they moved out to the more salubrious areas like Stanford Hill, Golders Green (now fondly nicknamed 'Goldberg Green'), Hackney and Tottenham. Their descendants are still there to this day living in all the bigger and better houses.

Italians

There's a little Italian community living around the borders of Clerkenwell and Holborn where St Peter's Italian Church sits. These are the descendants of the poor immigrants that had pitched up, again hoping to escape poverty, from Piedmont and Lombardy. (Remember the Lombard Street bankers?)

They lived in and around Hatton Gardens working as skilled clock-makers and also making instruments for measuring things. They later moved into other professions like picture-framing and organ-grinding. Practically all the street musicians that could be heard throughout London (making a God-awful racket) pushed their organs (and monkeys) out of the Clerkenwell area every day. Many of the grubby chestnut sellers we see around the West End are also descended from those early Italian settlers.

But the Italians were to become more famous for something else - ice cream, both making and selling. There were at one time 9,000 beautifully decorated ice-cream barrows leaving the Italian quarter every day. Immigrant Carlo Gatti made a fortune by importing bulk shipments of ice from Norway and producing literally tons of the stuff. As there were no fridges in those days, the ice was kept in deep pits (called ice wells) in the East End. Come to think of it, had there been fridges, they wouldn't have had to import ice anyway. Later the ice cream was taken round the streets on tricycles and the salesmen were called 'okey-pokey men'. (Hokey-pokey was an early name for ice cream.)

By the Way

Many of the ice-cream vans touring the inner suburbs still bear Italian sounding names (Notoriani, Della Mura, Mister Whippy(?)). They are mostly owned by descendants of those first immigrant families.

The Italian community was also responsible for figurine, ornamental statues and plasterwork which they produced from workshops in Soho and Fitzrovia (the area surrounding Charlotte Street). There are still a couple of specialist plasterwork shops (now rather naff) in Berwick Street, Soho, not to mention Tiranti's, the suppliers of everything to do with model-making, who still have a place in Fitzrovia.

These days we probably thank the Italians most for all the little restaurants that introduced Londoners, all that time ago, to a completely different (and cheap) style of cuisine. Typical were those opened by the Bertorelli brothers whose family still has its original restaurant in Charlotte Street.

By the Way

The Gatti family (of ice-cream fame) became even more rich by opening a chain of inexpensive restaurants and cafés that were eventually overshadowed by Lyons Tea Houses in 1894. They also ran a couple of music halls, one in Westminster Bridge Road (commonly known as Gatti's Over the Water) and the other at Charing Cross.

Chinese Crackers

London has had a Chinese population for hundreds of years, principally because of the Chinese seamen who settled in and around Limehouse (so called because it had once housed so many limekilns). It was a dark, mysterious and frightening place, full of opium and gambling dens and takeaways (sorry, that last one's not true) - a melting pot of seafaring lowlife from far and wide which lurked in a twilight world of rickety warehouses and dockland hovels. Londoners were advised to avoid Limehouse like the plague. In a short history of Limehouse by Daniel Lysons (1811) it was described thus:

In Limehouse on any day in the week one may meet strangers whose home address is in any corner of the seven seas. Lascars [Asian sailors] with slipshod gait, Malays and Chinese, turbaned Indians, full-blooded negroes, Scandinavians and West Indians, and curious composite creatures in frock coats and fezzes or dungarees and umbrellas, and every incongruous combination.

The Chinese colony, following the demise of London as a port, jumped in their rickshaws and moved to 'Chinatown' in Soho (hemmed in between Shaftesbury Avenue, Leicester Square and Charing Cross Road) where it flourishes to this day (although still a centre for drugs and gambling).

By the Way

If you visit Limehouse, be sure to call in at the beautiful St Anne's Church in Commercial Road. It was originally built between 1712 and 1724 and features the highest church clock in London. ('So what?' I hear you cry.)

A New House for Parliament

In 1834 London lost its Houses of Parliament in a fire. They were replaced by the ones we've got now, designed by Charles Barry (who liked the classical look) and his mate Augustus Pugin (who loved a more over-the-top Gothic style).

Their brief was to make it twice as big in only six years and for the ridiculously small sum of £80,000. It ended up taking twenty-five years, costing £2,000,000, and sending poor Pugin to a madhouse where he died aged only forty. Barry also died before the work was finished. Heigh-ho!

By the Way

The cruel Krauts destroyed the House of Commons again with their bombs during World War Two and it was rebuilt by Sir Giles Gilbert Scott between 1945 and 1950. Unfortunately, most of Pugin's brilliant, over-the-top decoration was simplified to the point of blandness.

By Another Way

Good news: the first ever gas-powered traffic signal was invented by J P Knight, a railway signalling engineer, and placed outside the Houses of Parliament. The bad news was that it blew up, killing a policeman.

Crime and Punishment

The massive influx of Jews and Irish meant that there were far too many people expected to live in London by honest means (there still are). There simply wasn't enough work. The government reckoned that if some restraint could be made on the Irish (in particular), robberies would be reduced overnight. If you're Irish, don't take offence - and don't blame me!

Nowhere was safe. In 1800, ships were disgorging 3,000,000 packages a year, and river pirates were managing to cream off £250,000s-worth, mostly from West Indian merchants. To be strictly fair, the pirates weren't the only ones in on the act: almost as much gear was disappearing due to the collusion of the watermen and watchmen.

The other great crime was counterfeiting coins, and at one time there were as many as fifty 'private' mints turning out dodgy dough. It was also calculated that half the hackney coachmen were 'flashmen'; that is, in league with, and in the pay of, thieves. Pickpockets were everywhere in the West End and were often indistinguishable, dress-wise, from the night-time theatre goers.

★ WORTH A VISIT? ★

If you are ever in the Newington Recreation Ground at Southwark, it might give you a bit of a thrill to realise that you are walking over the very site of the extremely nasty Horsemonger Lane Gaol, built in the 1790s. Charles Dickens attended the hangings of a couple who murdered a friend (some friend) for his money and then hid his remains under the floorboards (smelly or what!). He wrote in *The Times*:

> *I do not believe that any community can prosper when such a scene of horror as was enacted outside Horsemonger Lane Gaol is permitted. The horrors of the gibbet and of the crimes which brought the wretched murderers to it, faded in my mind before the atrocious bearing, looks and language of the assembled spectators.*

Everyone thinks of the Victorians as being puritanical but, underneath any veneer of genteel, prudish respectability, one usually finds a sewer of sleaze trying to get out (politicians take note). Pornography was all the rage in Victorian times and it was mostly concentrated in Holywell Street, which was buried when they built the Aldwych. In those days most of the rudest stuff was drawn by some of the best-known illustrators of the day. The market was simply enormous.

By the Way

Black-and-white-illustrators were regarded like super-stars in those pre-telly, pre-movie and pre-photo days - every middle-class household owning and enjoying many illustrated books and journals. There were several private clubs for these arty men-about-town. Two of them - the Langham Sketching Club and the London Sketch Club, where they entertained the stars of the day - are still in existence in Dilke Street, Chelsea.

Ladies of the Night

The Haymarket SW1 (known as Hell Corner) was the centre for prostitution in nineteenth-century London, and even outside the deeply respectable Bank of England, loose women were said to have stood in rows like hackney carriages. Many of the girls had other 'day jobs' - anything from hatters and trimmers, milliners, launderesses, servants, shop-girls and even fishwives. Even though there were thousands on the streets, it was claimed that demand always outstripped supply. Then there were the brothels all around the Soho area, which has remained the centre for that sort of thing right up to this day.

GET UP TO MUCH LAST NIGHT ?

But this was still the top end of the trade. If you'd have hung around places like Ratcliff Highway (St George St), Bluegate Fields or the wretched Shadwell* High Street (all in

* The Victorians' favourite colour was mauve and the aniline dye that produced it (the first synthetic one) was invented by William Perkins who lived in Shadwell.

the East End and now disappeared) you'd have seen creatures that would have made your flesh creep – the real bottom end of the trade. Tragic women in filthy clothes, their faces made hideous by the effects of smallpox, literally swigging gin in the gutters while trying to pick up 'rough trade'.

By the Way.

In 1857 it was estimated that one in every sixty houses in London (there were 6,000) was a brothel and that one in every sixteen women (there were 80,000) was 'on the game'.

Kids Involved

Saddest of all was the huge amount of child prostitution. This was partly because, for some unaccountable reason, sexual intercourse was supposed to cure inherited venereal disease. I'm no doctor but . . .

Talking of children, it should be noted that the largest proportion of the crime in London was down to them. To be honest, so many were neglected, disowned or exploited by their parents, that they had no option but to beg, borrow or steal simply to stay alive. It was commonplace for parents to send the kids out every day to see what they could find, whether it be from shops, pockets, or through open doorways or windows.

The bigger ones even used violence, particularly garrotting (strangling either with thumbs, knotted rope or a short stick) which reached epidemic proportions in the nineteenth century, being regarded by the criminal fraternity almost as an art form.

Famous Londoners No. 32: *Jack the Ripper*

All this violent crime came to a head in 1888 with the murders of women by a mysterious character nicknamed 'Jack the Ripper'. Polly Nichols, who lived (after a fashion) in a doss-house and serviced her addiction to gin by prostitution, was found with her throat and abdomen slit open in Buck's Row (now Durward Street). The next, Annie Chapman, was mutilated and decapitated.

More followed - all in the East End, and all chopped up rather expertly with a particular ultra-sharp knife. So good was the carving that the police thought it could well be the work of a doctor or surgeon (or at least a butcher). The murders, somewhat understandably, created total hysteria throughout the city with vigilante groups prowling the streets and picking on anyone who looked a bit suspicious (particularly foreigners and Jews). Eventually, over 600 plain clothes detectives were drafted onto the case. Needless to say, Mr Ripper was never found.

By the Way

The greatest breakthrough in the checking of London's soaring crime rate came by the rapid proliferation of back-street lighting, with whole areas being suddenly made safe from footpads and, worse, nasty men hiding in dark corners.

Famous Londoners No. 33: *Sarah Levenson*

If you're ever in Chappels, the music shop in New Bond Street, you might be interested to know that it used to be *Beautiful For Ever*, an incredibly posh cosmetic shop owned by the incredibly ugly Sarah Rachel Levenson. You could have bought 'The Royal Arabian Toilet of Beauty as arranged by

Madam Rachel for the Sultan of Turkey', or maybe 'The Dew of the Sahara' for removing wrinkles, all at prices ranging from 100 to 1,000 guineas. (Some wrinkles!)

Sarah had been a poor East End tavern fortune-teller in the 1840s when once, sick with a fever, she had all her hair chopped off in hospital. A doctor who supplied the remedy helped Sarah see what a doddle it would be to specialise in bogus treatments for all the things women worry about. By 1858 she was earning the ludicrous sum of £20,000 a year (around £820,000 in today's money).

She was eventually jailed for forging love-letters from Lord Ranelagh to a rather plain widow called Mrs Mary Borrowdale, just so's the old fraud could get Mrs B to part with a ludicrous £5,300 (£200,000) for treatments to make her prettier.

CHEAP TRAVEL FOR ALL

It must be generations since anyone but highbrows lived
in this cottage . . . I imagine most of the agricultural labourers
round here commute from London: Anthony Powell

At the beginning of the nineteenth century, roads throughout Britain were still pretty dreadful - rutted, unlit and dangerous, especially after dark. Making your way, therefore, through the country was painfully slow and although the first proper road surface was invented by John Macadam, and used in Bristol for the first time in 1815, it took ages to reach the rest of the highways and byways. The bigger cities were by now a nightmarish tangle of vehicles - from phaetons, to hansoms, to dogcarts, to landaus - not to mention all the by-products (to put it delicately) of those that pulled them. Good for the roses maybe, but no good for your shoes or the ladies' trailing skirts.

Something had to be done before this tangled knot of carts disappeared under a pile of aromatic horse-poo. Not only that, but travel through London wasn't that cheap either: there were tollgates everywhere - on most of the bridges coming into the city and at different locations as far apart as Notting Hill, Hackney, Holloway and Camberwell.

By the Way
At the height of the popularity of coach-travel, eighty-four coaches set out daily from the George and Boar in Holborn alone and fifty from the old White Horse Cellar in Piccadilly.

Rail Time
The first proper railways, with proper fare-paying customers,

opened in 1830 between Liverpool and Manchester. I wonder whether the poor horses that pulled up at the stations to drop off their passengers, realised that those heaving, panting machines would soon ring a death-knell, with nothing more for the horses than a short trip to the local knacker's yard or glue factory to look forward to.

It wasn't long (six years) before London had the first of its own passenger lines running between Deptford and London Bridge and then, a little later, further on to Greenwich.

By the Way

The authorities were so doubtful that this whole railway business was going to catch on and make money, that they charged those too nervous to try the train a penny to walk on the path beside the rails.

The first line running into London, came from Birmingham to Euston, in 1831, and it heralded a complex web, with London the big, fat spider in the middle. It meant that, relatively soon after (provided you had the dosh), you could travel anything up to 100 miles, to the capital, to do your shopping and be safely home the same day. Just imagine what that must have seemed like in times when even a journey of a few miles had seemed like a safari.

In the beginning, however, when these lines first hit London and sliced mercilessly into the city, the upheaval became something Londoners had never witnessed before. This is how Charles Dickens described it in *Dombey and Son*:

> *The first shock of a great earthquake had, just at that period, rent the whole neighbourhood to its centre. Traces of its course were visible on every side. Houses were knocked down; streets broken through and stopped; deep pits and trenches dug in the ground; enormous heaps of earth and clay thrown up; buildings that were undermined and shaking, propped by great beams of wood. Here a chaos of carts, overgrown and jumbled together, lay topsey-turvey at the bottom of a steep hill; there confused treasures of iron soaked and rusted in something that had accidentally become a pond. Everywhere there were bridges that led nowhere; thoroughfares that were wholly impassable; Babel towers wanting half their height; temporary wooden houses and enclosures, in the most unlikely situations; carcasses of ragged tenements, and fragments of unfinished walls and arches, and piles of scaffolding, and wildernesses of bricks, and giant forms of cranes, and tripods straddling across nothing.*

Crikey, old Charlie made it sound like the aftermath of an atomic bomb. Not surprising, the results were similar. Thousands of homes and shops were flattened to make room for these great iron snakes and they were mostly those occupied by poor tenants with damn-all claim for recompense. The railway companies, of course, were supposed to rehouse them but, then as now, how many times have you heard a railway company promise something and then not do it?

That first line into London had proved useless for commuters. Why? Because there were no stops between Harrow (way out in the country) and the centre. Harrow, by the way, is now just part of the great urban sprawl that carries on northwards practically to Watford. Travelling conditions were also pretty horrid, the carriages – little more than cattle trucks – being roofless and often without seats.

By the Way

The first tunnel was cut under Belsize Park NW3, because the posh and well-connected residents had the clout to make sure it wasn't going to go through their back yards. The men who did the digging (with no more than standard-issue buckets and spades) were descendants of the first Irish 'navvies' – or navigators – who'd been brought in to dig the canals.

What's The Time?

As the railways spread further and further afield, the operators realised that it might be quite a good idea to make the rest of Britain come into line with London, time-wise, for, without a standard time, timetables became a nonsense. (Until Greenwich Mean Time was established in 1884, most stations showed local time as well as London time). It's funny really, these days they'd be able to make that an excuse for all those trains that are never anywhere when you need them.

The rail network also made a proper Royal Mail service possible and in 1840 a penny-post was introduced with the very first postage stamps. Before then, the mail, which had relied on horsepower, had been slow and really expensive.

By the Way
London's newspapers, like *The Times*, the *Morning Chronicle* or the *Observer*, could also be on a breakfast table anywhere the railways went and, before long, telegraph poles shadowed the rails of the ever-widening system.

Over
By the 1860s loads of private railway companies from various parts of the land, thanks to the genius of Victorian engineers, were finding their way into the very heart of the city, building their own bridges across the Thames or carrying them over densely populated areas by means of lofty viaducts.

. . . and Under
Those early tunnels had obviously given them ideas, for in 1863 a railway dived mole-like beneath the ground for the four miles between Farringdon Street and Paddington. The modern Circle Line still follows the same path, and if you go to Platform 6 at Baker Street Station, you will notice that it's been preserved to look just as it did when it was built (grubby and covered in litter?). Then, as now, travelling on the first underground was a pretty dirty pastime, as there was nowhere for the soot-stained steam and black smoke to escape to.

The net result of all this easy access to the city was that those city workers who could afford the fares were able to move up to ten miles from the centre, and it was from this point that London's more salubrious (rich to you) suburbs were spawned. The poor, for obvious reasons, had to stay practically within walking distance of the docks, markets or building sites, until the government in 1883 forced the railway companies to offer cheap early morning fares. This, almost overnight, created working-class inner suburbs like Deptford, Walthamstow and West Ham (which they still are).

★ WORTH A VISIT? ★

It was at this time that the great steam stations were built, culminating in 1868 with Sir George Gilbert Scott's famous cross between a cathederal and Gothic fairy castle – St Pancras Station. It was the main terminal for the Midland Railway, and one of the true wonders of Victorian architecture (their equipment, by the way, was still, in today's terms, positively primitive). It was built originally as the now long-gone (1935) and utterly magnificent Midland Grand Hotel, with the train

station incorporated into it. These days, St Pancras's almost ludicrous pinnacles, towers and gables seem to be far too over-the-top for a mere station, but it remains to remind us of how our Victorian great-great-grandfathers went about things.

By the Way

Sir George Gilbert Scott also designed the hideous but quirky Albert Memorial.

By Another Way

Sad to say, the coming of the railways was to end Southwark's life as the southern gateway to London. All the old coaching inns closed down until only the George remained (see page 198).

Trams

Independent traffic had, as predicted, become mayhem, and so horse-drawn trams (which stuck to specific tracks and could take many passengers far more cheaply), were introduced. These were banned from the West End and the city, because those that controlled such things claimed that the traffic had become so heavy that anything that couldn't weave and twist would cause more problems than it would solve. Rubbish; the real reason was that trams would bring more working-class people into the city centre. Those in charge simply didn't want to lower the tone any further. The new trams eventually went out as far as Richmond to the west, Ponders End to the north and Streatham in the deep south. Presumably the East Enders still had to walk!

By the Way

By 1898 there were 1,451 trams pulled by a gang of 14,000 horses.

Here Comes the Motor Bus

The first motor buses in 1901, which were electrically propelled, were regarded as a massive joke by the short-sighted horse-drawn-bus drivers, as they kept breaking down and looked silly without a horse pulling them. The petrol buses, which followed, turned out to be almost as bad and it wasn't until three years later that The London General Omnibus Company ran its first regular service, with a steam driven single-decker bus, between Hammersmith and Piccadilly. This opened the floodgates for loads of new companies running a weird array of steam, electric and petrol coaches until the mayhem ended in 1908 with a standardised vehicle - the famous 'Old Bill', which soon became part of everyday London.

Birth of the Proper Suburb

These days it's very difficult to work out where London starts and ends, probably because all the little villages and towns, which were once surrounded by countryside, have now been swallowed up to become just a part of the Greater London suburbs. They now stretch up to twenty miles north, south, east and west.

The first real middle-class London suburb, at Bedford Park, Turnham Green (near Chiswick), now seems fairly central, but it was originally dumped fairly and squarely in the countryside. It was designed by the the Victorians' foremost architect, Norman Shaw, to be what became known as a 'garden suburb', with its own church, tennis-courts and even a mock-medieval inn (the Tabard). People all around laughed and ridiculed it as a haven for arty types.

The Birth of the Flat

Purpose-built flats or apartments had been known for years in many other major cities around Europe, but arrived fairly late in London. They were originally seen as a brilliant way of storing the poor, and the first were built in 1847 by the

Metropolitan Association, opposite the Old St Pancras Church. The MA was a charitable institution that didn't require a high return on its money. Each flat had a proper parlour, lavatory, piped water and a built-in kitchen range.

The first tenement blocks to give a warning of the hideous stuff we still see around us, were thrown up in Kings Cross, Covent Garden and Bethnal Green. These were remarkable as they were designed so that the put-upon-poor would live 'in a sanitary state'. (Patronising or what?) All the corridors were built with non-closing windows and the internal doors and windows to the flats were constructed specially to let in howling draughts – just so that there would be a good circulation of clean, healthy air. They obviously didn't want to make poor people too comfortable, otherwise they might have forgotten their place.

Even more bleak were the Peabody Buildings (which can still be seen), built with money squeezed out of the American philanthropist George Peabody. The first ones were built in Commercial Street, Spitalfields in 1862. They were pretty grim, but admittedly far, far better than the hideous rookeries that they replaced.

★ WORTH A VISIT? ★

The first super-smart apartment blocks for the rich were the wonderful six-storey Albert Hall Mansions (by the Albert Hall) built in 1870. These were designed in the 'Dutch Style', again by Norman Shaw, and included the very first lifts, along with beautiful bathrooms and wine cellars (a cellar in a flat?). Certainly not for the hoi polloi. Only recently I visited one that had not been touched internally since it was built. Great stuff!

Lav Alert

With all these extra people living, working and everything else-ing in London, something had to be done about the increasing nightmare of what to do with the tidal wave of sewage. At last someone came up with the brilliant idea of building a massive main sewer, alongside the river, to cut off all the smaller ones before they had a chance to spit their dubious contents into the Thames. Separate drains could then be built to take the clean rainwater straight into the river. They realised that in order to do this they'd have to tidy up the river's raggedy edge and it was then that they remembered an old idea of Christopher Wren's. By 1874 they'd incorporated the sewer into the magnificent sweeping 'Embankments' with their lovely plane trees, over-the-top but stylish cast-iron dolphin lamps and lion-headed mooring rings. The Embankments were probably the best thing the Victorians ever did for London.

By the Way

By building the embankments, the Victorian engineers reclaimed thirty-two acres of useless mud.

SHOWING OFF WITH THE VICTORIANS

London, the last beautiful city in the world:
Saturday Review 1856

Britain, and particularly London, was riding high, and throughout the world she was regarded with awe and respect. ('What went wrong?' I hear you cry.) Queen Victoria had fallen madly in love with a German Prince (in those days practically everyone in Germany was royal) called Albert Francis Augustus Charles Emmanuel of Saxe-Coburg-Gotha (Bertie for short). From the kick-off, the tall, rather gloomy consort did his level best to ingratiate himself with the English people by becoming more English (and more Victorian) than the English.

Prince Albert and his new chums wanted something really special to rub into foreigners' faces (especially the Germans'), to convince them how great and rich Britain had become and to make it clear that London really must now be regarded as the capital of Europe.

An Exhibition

They decided on a great exhibition to show off all we had achieved and what we were about to do (a bit like our wonderful Millennium Dome, but with something to boast about, and with something to put in it). They decided, in a flash of pure inspiration, to call it The Great Exhibition, which pleased little Victoria no end - she thought her precious Albert walked on water anyway. There were many opponents to the plan, some of whom thought that by encouraging all those people to congregate (especially filthy foreigners) it might bring about the next plague, or, even worse, that the blasted Catholics might see it as a golden opportunity to go round converting everybody.

By the Way

The stodgy old *Times* forecast that Hyde Park would become 'a bivouac of all vagabonds. Kensington and Belgravia would become uninhabitable and the Season* would be ruined'. How simply ghaaastly!!

The Big Greenhouse

The construction was organised by an illustrious committee including such mighties as Robert Stephenson (the train man), Isambard Brunel (the bridge man), William Cubitt (the builder man) and Charles Barry (the architect man). After squabbling over 245 designs they eventually chose an idea dreamt up by a little-known gardener and amateur architect, Joseph Paxton (he later helped do St Pancras), who scribbled his first sketch on a scrap of blotting-paper during his first visit to London. He'd been asked to have a go because he'd built a smashing glass conservatory for his boss, the Duke of Devonshire, at Chatsworth.

The truly magnificent thirty-metres-high 'Crystal Palace'

The 'Season' was, and still is, the series of lavish social and sporting events at which the top people meet and decide whom they're going to mate with.

was plonked slap in the middle of Hyde Park in the July of 1850, enclosing any trees that happened to get in its way. It was so big that it could easily hold the planned 14,000 exhibitors (largely British) and 100,000 exhibits (a 'galaxy of splendour'). The building was completed in an almost unbelievable four months (millennium dome-builders – hang your heads). Those Victorians certainly didn't hang about – for instance, the present Covent Garden Opera House only took them eight months.

By the Way

Londoners were so intrigued at the speed of the awe-inspiring, high-tech building-work that the cheeky contractors charged them five shillings-a-go to take a closer look.

By Another Way

When they enclosed the trees, they also enclosed all the sparrows, who, not being potty trained, did what sparrows still do – all over the precious exhibits. The doddery old Duke of Wellington, came up with the smart idea of introducing a couple of sparrow-hawks. The dirty little dickies departed *en masse* and *toute suite*.

What a Day

The little Queen thought the opening of the Great Exhibition 'the greatest day in our history' (she then turned up almost daily for three months), and, as far as the general public were concerned, it far outstripped any old royal wedding or funeral. London was in party mood for weeks, every hotel room was booked, city folk had their country rellies to stay, thousands slept out in the parks and 30,000 special guests were invited to the grand opening on 1st May 1851.

In the few months that it was open, 6,000,000 visitors each paid a shilling to get in (including an old lady of eighty-four who walked from Cornwall).

By the Way

Although it was supposed to be a showcase for Britain, visitors couldn't help noticing the ominously high quality of the goods from Germany, France and Belgium.

Exhibition Road

Of the £356,000 taken at the door of the Great Exhibition, £186,000 was used to buy a lot of land south of Kensington Road for £3,000 an acre (it must be worth telephone numbers these days) off an old boy called Baron de Graffenried Villars, a Swiss nobleman living in Paris. They then started building all the magnificent museums and Royal Colleges that are now London's pride and joy.

★ WORTH A VISIT? ★

All the museums are wonderful, but my vote has always gone to the Victoria and Albert, crammed full with everything to do with art and design. My favourite exhibit is in a glass case behind the massive statue of Michelangelo's *David*. It contains the plaster fig-leaf that they used to put over his ridiculously small willie when royalty was visiting.

And what happened to the Crystal Palace? It was bought by the Brighton

Railway Company, dismantled and moved to Sydenham, south London, where it became a leisure centre until it burned down in 1936.

Poor Do

Surely, at last, London could turn its back on its terrible reputation for ignoring the plight of the poor? In a way – yes, and in a way – no. Despite the unarguable success of the project and the huge amount of prestige Britain could now wave in front of the noses of its foreign neighbours, most of London's destitute could only look on with wavy smiles. The amount of new housing was certainly impressive, but not, unfortunately, as impressive as the massive population explosion – those Victorians sure were good at reproducing themselves.

Britain certainly led the world in science and technology, and had no trouble showing her competitors that she was not to be messed with when it came to our manufacturing industries, but what good was that to someone living and working in crappy, disgraceful conditions for ridiculously long hours, and being paid a mere pittance for their trouble? One only had to scratch just below the surface to realise that relatively few were becoming rich and comfortable at the expense and hard labour of the rest. There was still a whole side of British life which the Great Exhibition, and the wealthy Victorians, somehow forgot to mention.

In London, especially, there were still vast areas of abject poverty, with thousands living amongst filth and degradation. Jolly picturesque admittedly, when one views all those wonderful BBC Dickens adaptations, but not if you were one of the poor devils that had to endure it. In his great novel *Our Mutual Friend*, there is no better example of the savage contrast between those who had it and those who could only watch them enjoying it.

While the landed and well-heeled circulated in grand style amongst the posh ghettos of London's West End, and while superb hotels like Claridges and the Savoy, along with a score of gentlemen's clubs, catered to their, and their country equivalents' every need, the majority of its citizens could tell a different story.

River men still eked out a living by stripping and selling the dead bodies that were regularly pulled out of the stinking, misty Thames and from grovelling for discarded junk amongst

WELCOME ABOARD, SHIPMATE

the gloopy slime at the water's edge, while three generations of families were reduced to sifting through disgusting, dusty rubbish dumps for food or anything they could sell to buy enough to keep themselves alive for just one more day. Throughout the East End and all along the river, filthy, rat-infested streets pulsated with the dregs of humanity, all falling over each other simply to stay alive. John Hollingsworth, in his *Ragged London* (1868) claimed that London 'appeared to stagnate with a squalor peculiar to itself'.

★ Worth a Visit? ★

Should you find yourself stuck on the pedestrian island in the middle of the Euston Road (just under the sign to the A501), you will be on the site of the notorious Old King's Head Gin Palace, which was demolished in 1906.

Into a New Century

The twentieth century began in London with the mass hysteria and a massive drunken party in the West End following the relief of Mafeking in South Africa. On the 17th of May, news reached the capital that the British garrison besieged by the beastly Boers for six months had finally been reached and relieved by British troops. Hero of the hour was the man in charge Robert Baden-Powell. If the name's familiar, it was he who set up an organisation to show young city lads a better way of life. The Boy Scout movement grew from the first 20 in 1907 to 11,000 in two years.

Despite some observers labelling London rather grumpily as 'a cancer, a monster, a disease', it was still by far the most important city in the world bar none, with a population of 4,500,000 (five times what it had been in 1800) and still growing. The trade of the British Empire completely outshone that of the United States, Germany, France and Italy all together, and London's ports had had to swell just to cope with ten times the shipping of a century before. Londoners believed that their beloved city was unstoppable and, provided they weren't on the bread line, were justifiably proud of the old girl.

But a closer look would reveal that the icing was just beginning to slide off the top of the cake and London was beginning a slow, painful decline compared to other cities in the world which were, by this time, growing at an ever faster rate. Other nations were also beginning to catch up and in some cases outstrip Britain in production. London's elegant face was also being pockmarked with ugly new housing developments, office blocks and medium-priced hotels. Even Regent Street was stripped of all the lovely Nash detailing that had made it maybe the most beautiful street in the world. Posh areas like Mayfair and Belgravia were only just hanging on like grim death against the advances of the ever more entrepreneurial Edwardian property developers.

But London still pulsed with life and jollity - a sort of

unique spirit which, despite the abject poverty described earlier, couldn't then (and hopefully never will) be extinguished. The throbbing, tangled streets were a riot of colour, with literally scores of bus and tram companies, all in different livery, and all vying to get the pedestrians' bottoms on their seats.

There were very few chains of stores or restaurants in London at the beginning of the century, apart from a few like the Lyons teashops or their competition, the ABC (Aerated Bread Company) cafés, so generally each establishment still bore the name of the family that ran it.

At night time the upper classes didn't have it all their own way. Sure they had their Savoys, Café Royals and opera houses, but the ordinary folk also had five hundred bawdy music halls (with full dining facilities) like the Old Mo in Drury Lane, The Panorama in Shoreditch or Wilton's in Wellclose Square and, of course, the countless thousands of lively pubs.

By the Way

By the early part of the century the smaller music halls were being replaced by magnificently over the top variety palaces and the big stars of the day like Dan Leno, Marie Lloyd, Charles Colborn or Lottie Collins would have put the Spice Girls into the shadows famewise.

Cosmopolitan East End

As the twentieth century progressed, Stepney became a sort of magnet to Jewish, Russian and Polish immigrants fleeing from the nasty Nazis. Among them were little boys who were to become household names. They became men like Montague Burton from Lithuania, who was to head the massive menswear empire, Lew and Bernard Winogradsky from

Odessa, who, as Baron Grade and Baron Delfont of Bethnal Green, became probably the greatest theatrical impresarios ever. There was Charles Clore who became a top man in property, and many of the great entertainers of the 1930s and 1940s.

But the East End was first and foremost the home of the Cockneys, whoever they were and wherever they came from. Cockneys, of course, were fundamentally working-class but many became famous for their cocky, over-the-top, if slightly ragged at the edges, 'posh' clothing, as depicted in the famous music hall song 'Burlington Bertie from Bow' (Burlington referring to the ultra-smart Burlington Arcade in W1, and Bow being one of the poorest parts of the East End).

At the beginning of this century, the East End was a teeming melting-pot of these spirited, patriotic, self-opinionated, lovable but, most of all, tough human beings who were later to be terribly caricatured in the music halls and movies. Oddly enough, the real Cockney began to disappear as soon as his conditions began to improve. When all those filthy, rat-infested, back-to-back houses gave way to the impersonal apartment blocks that are so much a part of today's East End, the true spirit began to fade. Fings certainly weren't (and never would be again) what they used to be!

LONDON'S VERY OWN COUNCIL

London, the place you go to get bronchitis: Fran Lebowitz

At the end of the nineteenth century, London's gas, water, markets, docks and tramways were still under private ownership, and even a number of its parks and bridges; which meant you sometimes had to pay to cross the Thames or even take your dog for walkies. Everybody agreed that the administration, during the time of prime ministers Gladstone and Disraeli, had been pretty useless, especially for a city with such a massive population and international clout. The only answer was a council all of London's very own, to replace the creaking and corrupt Metropolitan Board of Works.

WHAT D'YOU MEAN - YOU AIN'T GOT ANY MONEY?

The London County Council was born in 1888 and lasted 77 years until it died in its sleep in favour of the (five times as big) Greater London Council. This new council, of 1888, had 126 councillors in charge of London's 117 square miles, 28 boroughs and 3,200,000 people, but the City proper remained a self-governing renegade – a sort of county in its own right.

The London County Council was the first metropolitan authority to be elected by Londoners themselves, with the various political parties practically tripping over each other (as they do now) to get overall control (the Liberals were in first).

Give 'em Houses

Before anything else, the new Council had to do something about the appalling conditions that London's poor were still having to endure. And they didn't hang about – by 1938 the council had built a stunning 86,000 new homes all over the city.

They then turned their attention to the problem of shifting all the people who lived in these places to work. Public transport was a shambles (and we all know what that feels like). The Council had to get the haphazard tramways into some sort of order, so they bought up all the private companies (whether they wanted to sell or not) and electrified them with overhead cables (the trams not the companies).

North-South Divide

One of their biggest problems was how to ease the increasing crush of traffic back and forth across the busy Thames every day. The beautiful Tower Bridge was opened in 1894 (for ages, the only crossing below London Bridge) to great hullabaloo, but despite this, and rebuilding and modernising six other bridges, it still wasn't enough. So, if going over the river wasn't the solution – it had to be under. In 1897 the new LCC opened the Blackwall Tunnel, in 1902 the Greenwich Tunnel, and in 1908 the Rotherhithe Tunnel.

By the Way

In the 1850s the City Steamboat Company of Battersea maintained loads of dear little paddle-boats shunting passengers up and down the river, but the CSC ran into financial trouble at the beginning of this century. Larger steamers chugged back and forth, carrying their cheery, Cockney cargoes between the Pool of

London and their favourite holiday resorts of Southend and Margate, on the Kent and Essex coasts, right up till the 1950s.

Despite numerous, usually underfinanced, attempts over recent years, the river must now be one of the most underused in any major city. A once brilliant and busy thoroughfare (once compared to Venice) is now ignored by government and entrepreneur alike. All this at a time when London's main arteries are so blocked with motor traffic that a seizure seems imminent.

★ WORTH A VISIT? ★

A real North-to-South, South-to-North traffic speeder-upper was the Kingsway-Aldwych scheme, built in 1905. You can still see the rather spooky, long-shut-off remains of the cobbled tram tunnel disappearing into nowhere at the top of Kingsway WC2.

CAN WE HAVE
OUR MARBLES
BACK?

By the Way

The top end of the Kingsway tunnel (the closed bit) was used to store and protect the priceless Elgin marbles against damage from the gruesome German bombing during the Second World War. Good idea. It was so nice to see that we were taking such good care of the treasures we'd nicked off the Greeks in the first place.

Busy Schedule

Next, the London County Council scrapped the old School Boards and, in 1930, took over all the Poor Law infirmaries making them into a proper hospital service with 40,000 beds. Three out of every four beds were now supplied by the LCC.

By 1925 the LCC was on a roll. With a huge budget of £23,000,000, these were some of its responsibilities:

Licensing239lodgings166slaughterhouses130cowhouses355 offensivebusinesses(whateverthatmeans)maintaining966elementary schoolswith700000pupils259technicalandeveningschoolsemploying 23500teachersrunning160milesoftramwayscarrying700000000 passengersayearlookingafter10bridgesand4tunnelstheWoolwichfree ferry115parksmaintainingthefirebrigade66trainstationsandthe LondonAmbulanceServicesupervisingthesafetyof655theatresmusic hallsandcinemasmaintaining10mentalhospitalsproviding347cricket pitches436footballpitchesand713tenniscourtsregistering800 employmentagenciesand…720massageparlours.

Now close your eyes, and repeat the list to see if you've been paying attention.

The Salubrious Suburbs?

As all that public housing was being thrown up to house the poor in the inner city, it was almost equally matched by all the private development in the suburbs which was spreading like a huge web with London like a fat spider in the centre. All this had been made far more possible now there was some decent transport in the form of railways, electric tramways and, later, trolleybuses to bring the workers into its heart. By 1930 commuters were coming in from as far apart as Epsom, Windsor, Bishop's Stortford and Hatfield.

... and Underground

Most successful of all was the ever-growing underground system which was spreading under the city in ever-widening circles. By 1901 the Circle Line was finished and electrified and this allowed a round tour of London (albeit in the gloom) of fifty minutes. But these first lines were dug from the surface and then covered over, which, as you might imagine, caused real problems in planning and a mass of urban demolition. When they invented a method of deep boring (deeply boring), using massive underground tubes, they were able to go where they damn well pleased, like deranged moles, without even having to think about what was going on on the surface. It was when all these lines - the District, Bakerloo, Piccadilly, and Hampstead (later to become part of the Northern line) - joined up that the whole thing began to take on a semblance of what it is today.

Metroland

By far the most famous of all the railway developments, however, was the Metropolitan Railway; two lines which snaked out to Watford and Amersham. The Metropolitan opened up huge suburbs like Wembley, Harrow, Pinner, Chorley Wood and Uxbridge, all to be labelled, by the canny property developers, Metropolitan Country Estates - 'Metroland'.

But it wasn't just the railways that had had to improve. There was a huge expansion in road building throughout the suburbs, with wide highways, like the now hideous Western Avenue, which bulldozes its way right to the centre, and the even

WARNING
YOU ARE JOINING THE NORTH CIRCULAR

more hideous North and South Circulars. These made it possible to drive from one side of the city to the other without being caught up in the centre. In 1911 the average Londoner took 210 rides on some form of public transport or other. By 1939 it was double that.

Behind the Green Belt.

All this expansion was all very well, but London's planners had bigger ideas. They wanted new, smallish, self-sufficient towns to take the strain off the city. The controversial Garden Cities were plonked often clumsily in the vast 'Green Belt' that surrounded London. This was the beginning of Welwyn and Letchworth, and then Milton Keynes, Stevenage and Crawley. It all seemed ideal at first, but the problems came thick and fast.

For a start the new towns, who could pick and choose whom they wanted, would only accept skilled workers, which meant that the rest had to stay in the crowded conditions of inner London. The new town corporations then tempted London-based industries to follow their skilled workers by offers of almost silly cut-price deals on brand-new factories, which resulted in those unskilled workers who did have jobs, having nowhere to be unskilled in. That, with the beginning of the end of the docks, indicated a pretty gloomy future for the poor working-class Londoner.

TROUBLE AHEAD

The people of London with one voice would say to Hitler,
'You have commited every crime under the sun . . . we will have
no truce or parley with you.': Winston Churchill 1941

If London's working men were having it bad, London's womenfolk were having it worse. They'd had just about enough of being treated as second – or maybe third – class citizens. They weren't even allowed to vote – can you imagine that? The Women's Social and Political Union, or as the *Daily Mail* labelled them, the Suffragettes, marched down to hit London, from their base in Manchester, in 1906.

These dames weren't daft, however – just tough. They were well aware that, if, for one minute, they believed they could make the politicians listen by going through the normal, respectable channels, they might as well roll over on their backs and think of England (as women had done for centuries). Headlines were what were needed – and fast: so they proceeded to titillate the popular press like the ban-the-bombers of the sixties. These outwardly respectable, demure-looking ladies (all long black frocks and bonnets) proceeded to smash windows, slash famous paintings, like Velasquez's best nude, the *Rokeby Venus* (she's still got the stitches), chain themselves to railings, plant bombs in St Paul's Cathedral, disrupt the Opera at Covent Garden with megaphones (appropriately during *Joan of Arc*) and one of

them even killed herself by jumping in front of the King's horse on Derby Day - a touch drastic, but guaranteed to get the front page.

Surprise, surprise, all of this had less than no effect on the all-male, all-chauvinist powers that be (or were), but I'm delighted to report that those pompous old bu. . .ffers (with copious egg-on-face) were later forced to give in, when even *they* had to recognise the staggering work that the womenfolk had done in the First World War (coming next). In 1918 women over thirty were given full voting rights.

★ WORTH A VISIT? ★

One of the most famous events of the early twentieth century was the 'Siege of Sydney Street' in 1911. A gang of jewel thieves, thought to include the infamous anarchist Peter the Painter, was tracked down to a house in Sydney Street, in the East End, and surrounded by police marksmen. They exchanged bullets for five hours until (oddly) the house caught fire and, before the fire brigade could put it out, everyone inside was burned to death. Many famous Londoners turned up to watch, including Winston Churchill and my granddad (see page 2) who was one of the firemen in attendance.

War Breaks Out

If the young men of Britain had only known how the future was to pan out, they would never have rushed to the recruiting-stations like frisky lambs to the slaughter when the announcement was made in August 1914 that we were at war with Germany.★

★ *There was no compulsory call to arms.*

At last they had a chance to show the arrogant, strutting Hun what we Brits were made of. 'It'll all be over by Christmas,' they chortled, 'once they feel the cold steel of our British bayonets.'

London became caught up with conflict as if it was an elaborate faraway game and, for four years, while her brave (if a little naive) young men were being mercilessly slaughtered in their thousands on the ghastly battlefields of France and Belgium, the city became almost maniacally merry.

Anyone remotely German was, of course, rounded up and put in prison, and even anyone with a vaguely foreign-sounding name was given a real hard time (even if the country they came from was on our side).

It was only when, on a beautiful clear morning in June, fourteen German planes appeared over London, that the city-dwellers began to take the whole business a bit more seriously. By the time those fiendish Fokkers* had left, 130 men, women and children were dead – 19 of them innocent kids from North Street School, Poplar. After 25 raids and 900 bombs (which destroyed areas as far apart as Bethnal Green and Sydenham), the somewhat complacent Londoners, who lived in a city that had not been attacked for hundreds of years, finally realised that the Channel was no longer the ultra-wide moat that had previously deterred the would-be intruder. Having said that, no enemy soldier since William the Conqueror's merry men, has set foot in the city as an invader (unless you count those entangled in parachutes, shot down while trying to bomb us).

* *German bombers*

After the War was Over

As suggested in the last chapter, the population of Inner London was tumbling in inverse proportion to the growth of the suburbs. Nearly 400,000 were decanted to the new housing developments that were mutating and devouring our green and pleasant countryside like ravenous monsters. Just about all the major industries moved out too - Ford to Dagenham, the British film industry to Elstree and Pinewood, De Havilland the plane maker to Edgeware, Gillette and Hoover to Greenford - to name but a few.

But while the inner London working man bemoaned a lack of industry and the dole queues grew, London's rich, many of whom had profited nicely through the war, had a high old time with their hyper-posh hotels like the Ritz and the Dorchester, and super-stores like Harrods and Whiteleys, all anxious to ease them from their not very hard-earned cash. Park Lane became so flashy that it even showed signs of apeing New York and, most probably, would have done so, had there not been a new law passed restricting the height of buildings to twenty-four metres.

CAN YOU SMELL ANYTHING?

★ WORTH A VISIT? ★

If by any chance you are in the reception lounge of Shell-Mex House in the Strand WC2, and happen to catch a faint whiff of horse-poo - be not concerned. You are actually standing in the old horse-and-carriage-park for the Hotel Cecil (demolished in 1930), once the largest hotel in the world.

By the Way

Domestic service still accounted for the largest proportion of the workforce in London after the war. The Great British (lower) Middle Class and Non-servant Class was still only just emerging from the womb.

Slump Time

Despite another great attempt to show the rest of the world how brilliant we were, the hugely successful British Empire Exhibition in 1924 heralded a massive recession which badly hit Britain and London (and the East End of London in particular). The inevitable General Strike of 1926 was sparked off by the miners who'd been locked out of their beloved pits, but soon became a direct punch-up between the workforce and the Conservative Government.

For nine nail-biting days, anarchy ruled in London, as the police and army tried to protect members of the public who were trying to keep all the public amenities from seizing up, from the furious workers. The strike collapsed when the leaders of the revolt realised how futile it was to take on the might of the Government. It mattered little in the end, as the whole world was teetering on the edge of an economic slump that was to dominate the thirties.

★ WORTH A VISIT? ★

Architecture after the war was bright, hopeful and distinctive. Perhaps the most beautiful example is Wallis Gilbert's 1932 Hoover factory, on the Western Avenue, Perivale, which looks like a Hollywood film studio. Why don't you go there to do your shopping? Not for a vacuum cleaner: the factory is now a massive Tesco.

War No. 2

In Germany, that horrid little painter and decorator with the bad hair and silly moustache, Adolf Hitler, was giving his best to his hysterical followers. It soon became obvious that the idea of controlling London, still the most powerful city in the world, was what kept him awake at night (along with girlfriend Eva Braun).

When our wimpy little Neville Chamberlain told us, in so many words, that that nasty Mr Hitler not only wouldn't give us our ball back, but wouldn't withdraw from Poland and that we were unfortunately at war with Germany, Londoners hung around in an uneasy calm, waiting for something to happen. 89,000 children, pregnant mums and blind people from the London slums were shipped out of the city to their rather smart (and rather shocked) country cousins. Windows were blacked out, shelters (2,250,000 supplied by the Government) dug into back gardens, trenches dug in the parks, iron railings torn down to make weapons, doorways sandbagged, huge silver barrage balloons hoisted over the city centre, and food and luxuries rationed in preparation for the dark days ahead.

By the Way

Road deaths doubled owing to the new regulations which

ordered that all vehicles be driven with a single masked headlight.

Three defence lines were prepared by the Army and our dear little Home Guard: the outer one was quite a long way out, circling the suburbs from Rickmansworth to the north and Bromley to the south; the middle one linked northern Harrow with southern Norwood; the innermost one used the Thames as a southern limit, and the Lea and the Brent to the east and west. Our very best soldiers, the Royal Marines, were to be deployed to Whitehall if ever those Krauts crossed the Thames.

By the Way

Gun emplacements were disguised as tea kiosks in the heart of the city.

The Long Wait

But, for weeks and weeks, life went on as usual – talk about an anticlimax! Soon everyone began to relax; cinemas and theatres opened for business again and half the Cockney evacuees who'd hated all the fresh air and healthy living of the country (and sharing space with 'toffs') drifted back to their homes. But if the Boches weren't quite ready for us, they certainly were giving it plenty across the water. Scandinavia and the Low Countries had been invaded, and France, only a Channel swim away, had put up its hands and surrendered.

Britain's 'phoney' war lasted over a year until, on 7th September 1940, for the second time in the century, German bombers (this time 400 at a time) dropped their deadly cargo on poor old London. Those Germans just didn't fight fair, either. We'd expected them to arrive in the daytime, like nice, reasonable enemies, but the tricky devils came at night when we couldn't see them. In the week that followed, 1,400 incendiary bombs and 1,000 tons of explosives were dumped on the city.

It was to be London's worst and finest hour. There's nothing like adversity to bring people of all classes together, and London's were no exception. Rich and poor (150,000 of 'em) rushed to shelter in the Underground where they camped on the platforms and in all the linking tunnels. The unused tunnels were used as bomb-proof storerooms. In 1940 there was a direct hit on Balham station (which still looks like a bomb's just hit it); sixty-eight people were killed.

London's spirit was kindled by the very flames that engulfed her, and it soon became plain that whatever old Jerry managed to inflict on us, they could never beat it out of her. On 12th October, the penny (or should I say Deutschmark?) dropped, and a rather puzzled Hitler, harassed by our brilliant RAF, and the almost ridiculous resistance of the Londoners, gave up trying to invade, but continued to blitz the city, night after night (after night). By December, the Germans were dropping 8,000 bombs a night on a punch-drunk London, but still the old girl refused to roll over and play dead.

★ WORTH A VISIT? ★

In 1938, at the instigation of Sir Winston Churchill, the basements of the Civil Service building, between King Charles St and Parliament Square, were converted and reinforced to make the Cabinet War Office. It had the first direct telephone line to enable 'Winnie' to chat directly with the American president.

Devastation

It must be said, however, that the Germans had managed to do more damage than the Great Fire all those years earlier. London was trashed admittedly but, miraculously, there in the very centre, surrounded by total chaos, almost undamaged, and still showing the Germans the traditional two fingers (in the nicest possible way), stood St Paul's Cathedral – a magnificent symbol of the plucky Londoners' determined resistance. The height of the blitz came on 10th May 1941 when 1,436 people were killed right across the city. By the time the bombing ended, in 1944, 30,000 brave people were dead. Tragic, admittedly, but only a fraction of what had been predicted.

Doodlebugs

But that wasn't the end. Just as Londoners were trying to get some sort of life together, Hitler came up with a new weapon that he was sure would finally bring the city to its knees. The V1 or 'doodlebug' was a pilotless rocketship, way ahead of its time, that could cross the Channel all on its very own without some pilot to show it the way. It exploded on impact, but because the engines cut out when near its target, nobody knew quite where the target was. The eerie silence that followed its eerie engine noise was dreaded by every person who remained in the city.

By the Way

Our super-brave young pilots had become so skilled at Spitfire-flying that they learned to intercept many of the VIs by flipping them into another direction with their wings.

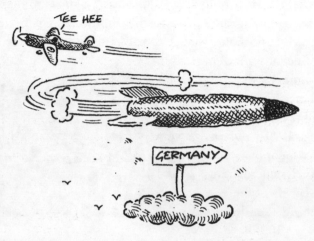

By the time the doodlebug launch-sites in the Netherlands were destroyed, and Germany had held up its bloodstained hands in surrender, one third of our city was as flat as a pancake, hundreds of thousands were homeless, thousands were dead and injured but ... London had won its finest victory. The massive party on VE Day, 8th May 1945, was apparently the very wildest ever (which was proved by the birth rate which, somewhat predictably, soared nine months later).

FIGHTING THE PEACE

It is not the walls that make the city, but the people who live within them. The walls of London may be battered, but the spirit of the Londoner stands resolute and undismayed:
King George VI

Britain had won the war and the Hun was handsomely humiliated, thanks to my dad who'd watched out for the bombers on a city roof and also, I suppose, all those other dads who'd actually fought in the war. But the peace that followed offered new problems. London, tired but unbowed, slid gently back into its old ways.

Uniforms and army memorabilia were stowed in hundreds of attics or under the stairs; scruffy, overgrown lawns were mown and hedges clipped as neatly as before, mothers went back to being the family's servant, providing Sunday lunch while listening to *Family Favourites* on the radio; holidays were planned at all those seaside resorts which again flourished as in the old days; and the East End pubs that hadn't been given a permanent closing time by Hitler's bombers were once more full to bursting on pay-days.

It was all just as before but, in a funny way, different. For once, in practically the whole history of the city, the rich and poor, through shared hardship and incredible selfless bravery, had gained a genuine respect for each other. This was a sentiment that was to last for years (until Thatcher and her irksome ilk went and put their well-shod feet in it). Also, the Royal Family surfed on a sea of popularity that hadn't been seen for years - probably because King George VI and Queen Elizabeth (our Queen Mum) had chosen to stay at home instead of scarpering off, like the rest of them, when the bombing got uncomfortably close.

Where to Live?

Unlike the railways, all those years before, bombers weren't known to check a person's standing in society before destroying his house, so rich and poor alike found themselves homeless. Unfortunately, it must be said, the poor did tend to get what they were given, while the better-off seemed to have an element of choice. Either way, the authorities didn't hang around, and promptly kicked off a massive rebuilding programme straightaway. The bomb-scarred East End became a no-man's-land of admittedly new, but dismal, faceless, uniform estates - the slums of the future. Many thought that by replacing mile upon mile of grimy back-to-back houses, Jewish shops, gin palaces, street musicians and the gutters for snotty, grimy-kneed children to play in, it would make for a brighter happier environment. History, sadly, tells us that those were the very ingredients that had made the East End of London the vibrant society it had been for years.

Let Them Live High

The silly authorities, who never seem to ask the people who count what they actually want, thought that high was beautiful, and many multi-storey monsters were thrown up to house the poor. I think the planners and architects should have been locked up in homes for the aesthetically bewildered. Not only did they think that the monsters looked good, but also that those jolly Cockney folk would fall over themselves to live in them, especially as they had recently left their sprawling, labyrnthine ghettos. But, as we know, that was far from the case, and only now are the powers that be beginning to pull down those disastrous dinosaurs, creating once more, little village-like developments of people-sized houses, with little backyards separated by fences over which Mum can gossip about ''er down the road', and sheds for Dad to keep his pigeons and fishing-rods in.

I WAS THINKING OF VISITING THE GROUND TODAY

By the Way

One of these awful buildings, Ronan Point in East London (admittedly built later) couldn't wait to be pulled down and collapsed of its own accord in 1968. Shoddy workmanship was to blame.

I DIDN'T TOUCH THE PLACE

ACME DEMOLITION

RONAN POINT

Festival Time

By the late forties it was time to shake off the gloom and show off a bit. First, in 1948, we staged the Olympic Games in our still-sensational Wembley Stadium and then, exactly a hundred years after the Great Exhibition (1851), Londoners were given a jubilant Festival of Britain dubbed 'a Tonic to the Nation', to tell the world that the old girl was off her knees and dancing again.

The Festival Committee decided to centre it on a vast area of bombsites east of Waterloo Bridge, and it was there that they constructed the controversial, but hugely successful, concrete Festival Hall complex (you either love it, or you hate it). They also made a fabulous pleasure ground and funfair in Battersea Park. I remember my mum and dad taking me there when I was knee-high, and can still recall the big-dipper, the walkways through the illuminated trees and the amazing dome★ that housed the best of what Britain could produce, all decked out in that clean, bright, primary-coloured, optimistic, spikey style that was to become the trade mark of the era.

Telly Time

I also remember my mum and dad buying a television (the first in our street) in 1953, so's we could watch our young and surprisingly pretty Queen marrying her Greek Prince Philipopodopoulos. It was watched by 20,000,000 (most of them on ours, as I remember), and the telly became the greatest growth industry after the war.

By the Way

Televisions were huge, ugly, cumbersome things in those days, with weeny little screens in the middle (sounds like the Telly

★ *'Don't mention domes,' I hear you cry.*

Tubbies). Most viewers opted for a huge, oil-filled magnifying glass in front of the screen, to make the picture bigger, and sometimes a ludicrous piece of clear plastic with blue at the top, pink in the middle, and green at the bottom, designed to make it look like colour.

By the Way (again)
It didn't!

Cars and Planes
Before the war, the family car had been a luxury that few could afford. Anyway, they were really boring-looking, based on the angular old designs of the twenties and thirties. American-owned Ford of Dagenham looked across to the States and started producing much sleeker, economical, baby versions of their big, flashy, Yankee brothers. Owing to many families having well over double the disposable income of before the war, the London streets were soon buzzing with Populars, Prefects, Consuls and top-of-the range Zodiacs. Streets that had once been empty, apart from the odd grocer's bike or horse-drawn milk float, began to fill up with parked cars.

London Airport (Heathrow) suddenly took off (sorry!) as cheaper flights and higher incomes made foreign travel possible to a whole section of the community that hadn't yet been further than Bognor or Brighton. Torremolinos and other resorts, soon to be hideously Anglicised, were to take on the characteristics of Southend.

New Faces

As one bunch was leaving, a whole new lot of people were arriving in the city (but not on holiday). A fresh wave of immigrants, particularly from the West Indies, who had traditionally preferred America were now being forced to come to London. The States had closed its doors in 1952. The number of immigrants to Britain soared from 1,000 to 20,000 in a year.

Despite stories to the contrary, the Mayor of Brixton welcomed them with open arms (and a big tea party), and so did London Transport and the hospital services, all of who were crying out for cheap labour. This, as you might imagine, shortly led to trouble. The capital's old-timers, who hadn't wanted to do those jobs anyway, became well-miffed when the Afro-Caribbeans, who assimilated well, began to rise above the sub-working class that they'd been forced into. In 1958 race riots exploded on the streets in the now quite posh Notting Hill area, which had, in only a few years, become largely a Jamaican community.

. . . and Asians

The other new faces that later appeared in the city were all the Asians who'd been thrown out of Kenya and Uganda. Punjabi Sikhs preferred Southall (which is now like Delhi High Street) mostly because they could get loads of work, admittedly badly paid, at nearby London Airport. The Bengali Muslims centred on Brick Lane, where they toiled in the thousands of sweat shops that produced the country's cheaper clothing.

Best of all, Asians brought with them particular talents, one of which was small-scale general storekeeping. The ubiquitous, open-all-hours Asian corner-shop has now become part of the fabric of London life, despite being resented by the very (stupid) people who patronise them most.

THEY'LL SOON BE TAKING US OVER, MRS SMITH. YOU MARK MY WORDS

PATEL

. . . and Greeks

The only other community that came to London in big numbers was composed of Greeks and Greek Cypriots and settled in Camden Town, Finsbury Park and the Fitzrovia parts of London (and one of them in Buckingham Palace). They, too, have added another great dimension to our city, with their ability to run daft, noisy restaurants, barber shops (why are all barbers called Tony?) and the very down-market clothing manufacturers that employ the Asians.

Baby Time

By the late-fifties, the result of all that relieved post-war nookie was teenagers - millions of 'em. Their world, for once not overshadowed by the threat of war (apart from Vietnam) or rationing, was only to be enjoyed. Their bright, optimistic music upset Mum and Dad (who constantly reminded them that they wouldn't be alive, save for what their parents had done in the war); their colourful clothes gave their post-Victorian grandma 'one of her turns'; art schools and colleges were sparkling, creative and anarchic (as they aren't now) and, by the time the sixties arrived, London's young were running the showdown.

THE SIZZLING SIXTIES

I love London. It is the most swinging city in the world at the moment:
B. Hillier 1965 (first ever reference to Swinging London)

The City that had once been 'London', had risen high above the bomb-sited, bind-weed-strewn ghost town of the fifties, but now had hardly any residents at all, once the 400,000 office workers took their tubes and buses home. Inner London's population was also still leaking badly into the suburbs due to the continuing movement out of the centre by industry. This continued right through the sixties.

Attempts over the last three decades to repopulate have been a moderate success. There's the massive but ugly Barbican site (finished in 1982) and, close by, the often beautiful conversions of waterside warehouses. These, together with the gentrification of the docklands to the east, are proving that London can be once more a city fit for people (albeit very rich people) to live in.

Elsewhere, staggeringly ugly buildings that only their creators - the architects - could love, have sprung up all over the shop. Some, like the monstrous Centre Point at the junction of Oxford Street and Tottenham Court Road, stayed empty for years and years (from brand new) because it was proved

AT LEAST IT'S
EASY TO
KEEP CLEAN

financially beneficial, owing to soaring land and property values (and the fact that you don't have to pay rates on empty buildings).

Here Comes the GLC

In the mid-sixties, Tory Prime Minister Harold Macmillan became fed up with having the London County Council continually controlled by Labour and replaced it with the Greater London Council. The theory (largely misplaced) was that if he included the more prosperous, Conservative-voting, outer suburbs, there'd be a much greater chance of the Tories gaining control.* To be fair, it also made far more sense, because, since the LCC was set up in 1889, the built-up area had spread right out to the Green Belt. The new GLC would take in 610 square miles – five times the area of the old LCC. One of the great problems with this new, larger Greater London Council was that it soon became clear that the more prosperous boroughs would be forced to pay through the nose to subsidise the poorer ones, which they didn't like one little bit. Funny that!

Wind of Change

London was changing rapidly in other ways. It was becoming more, how shall we say, 'foreign'. Teashops were giving way to espresso bars; the famous Lyon's Corner Houses were losing out to American-style hamburger and fried chicken chains; and there were as many Chinese, Italian, Greek and Indian restaurants as you could shake a knife, fork or chopstick at. Pubs even started that still-annoying habit of selling tea and

*It's interesting to note that, when this didn't happen, the government sneakily nibbled away at the GLC's powers under the guise of 'necessary administrative reforms'.

coffee and playing the sort of sloppy background music that is guaranteed to put you off your pint.

Here come the Mods

While the art students and 'Bohemians' inhabited the countless gloomy jazz clubs, gyrating to the (thankfully) now passé traditional jazz or turgid Bob Dylan look- and sound-alikes, the streets of London were vibrating to the high-pitched din of a form of transport that was to start one of the largest teenage cults ever.

Italian motor-scooters (Vespas or Lambrettas) were the rather unlikely and almost sissy steeds of the 'Mods'. These snappily-dressed young men and the less flamboyant females of the species, buzzed round the suburbs in hornet-like herds seeking out their sworn enemies - the 'Rockers' - sad, greasy, motor-biking throwbacks who worshipped American rock-a-billy music and congregated in the trashy transport cafés that ringed the centre of London (before going home to their mums). The Mods' musical idols were groups like the Yardbirds, the Who and the Small Faces and, strange as it may now seem, the Blue Beat and Ska that had emerged from our fairly newly arrived West Indian brothers and sisters.

By the Way

It's interesting to reflect that there was practically no racism amongst London's youth in the sixties. It was largely promoted by their bigoted (or more probably scared) parents and grandparents.

London Takes Off

The mid-sixties became a time when young people suddenly decided to do their own thing and ask big questions about the way their parents carried on (instead of the other way round). For the first time in years, Britain's teenagers (a relatively new term) weren't threatened by war - unless you counted the Third World tiff in somewhere called Vietnam, that didn't remotely concern them. For the first time, they had a bit of money of their own and, for the first time, there was a real alternative to alcohol if they wanted to get high ... pills! Few could deny that, for better or worse, London was the centre of the whole business.

The whole 'London Thing' exploded with a group of designers like Mary Quant, Barbara Hulaniki and John Stevens, who opened the somewhat naffly labelled 'boutiques' on soon-to-be-famous Carnaby Street and the King's Road. There were skirts so short they took your parents' breath away, ludicrous flared trousers with floral inserts, ankle-snapping stacked shoes and garish, acidic colours guaranteed to scare poor grannie.

The media dived in head first and hyped it to within an inch of its life. Soon 'Swinging London' became the mecca for the young and trendy, and if you weren't seen on the King's Road on a Saturday afternoon, you just weren't 'with it'. The trouble was, as most of us who were around at the time realised, however hard we tried, we never really knew what or where 'it' actually was. Many believe that Swinging London only really existed in a cluster of rather soppy films like *Blow Up* and *The Knack*.

★ WORTH A VISIT? ★

If you feel like sitting where we all sat in the sixties, watching the pageant go by (and sometimes being part of it), try the Picasso café halfway up the King's Road.

To confuse matters more, a new craze was creeping in from America, a gift from all those long-haired, dope-smoking drop-outs from the ever-escalating Vietnam War (that by now we all knew about). Suddenly, everywhere you looked, boys and girls were wearing identical tie-dyed cheese-cloth shirts, loose baggy trousers, soppy headbands, neckfuls of ethnic jewellery and horrible embroidered accessories proclaiming 'Peace' and 'Love' to all. It was all a load of media whipped-up nonsense, a fashion craze dressed up as an intellectual movement - in other words - bloody marvellous!!

Gang Rule

While the young were getting on with having a good time, London's underworld was playing a very different game. Sicily and New York had their Mafia, Hong Kong had its Triads, and London had a few gangs that kept control of all organised crime. Most notorious of all was the East End 'firm' run by the legendary Kray brothers - Ronnie and Reggie - who operated out of the Blind Beggar Pub.

★ WORTH A VISIT? ★

If you fancy a drink and want to drink in the atmosphere of villainy at the same time, visit the Blind Beggar (much, much calmer now) on the Whitechapel Road. It was the Krays' local and the 'boozer' where Ronnie shot rival George Cornell in broad daylight.

The vicious Krays controlled a large percentage of the East London underworld, running a vast 'protection' racket that worked on the quaint and simple basis that anyone not completely satisfied with their not-exactly-asked-for services was promptly shot, stabbed or worse. From 'protecting' second-hand car dealers and pub owners, they moved on to West End clubs and gambling dens, even opening some of their own in upmarket Kensington and Mayfair.

Then, from the protection game, the cunning Kray boys expanded into fraud, intimidation, drugs and pornography; but their main obsession was a rival gang called the Richardsons who 'ran' South London. Open warfare between the two mobs flared in 1966, and there followed a few years of sheer headline-grabbing terror and inter-gang massacre before the twins were finally arrested and sent down for a minimum of thirty years each. Ronnie, a homosexual, died in prison in 1995, but Reggie, bless 'im, is still doing his porridge. He is reputedly as mad as a snake and receiving twenty fan letters every day.

Neighbourhood Watch?

Oddly enough the gang system tended, if anything, to help keep small-time crime and violence off the London streets, and it was noted that when the big players, who were often thought of as 'thorough gents' were removed from circulation, the incidents of robbery and muggings rose considerably.

These gangs, you see, had a strange, twisted morality that rated snatching the purse off an old lady, or injuring a pet, far worse than torturing then executing a rival gang member. They ran a sort of self-policing operation in the areas they covered, a Neighbourhood Watch with teeth (and guns, knives and knuckle-dusters). Rather charming - in a macabre way.

The decline of gangs like the Krays' echoed the decline of the East End, whose population shrank from 900,000 in 1880 to 140,000 in 1980. This was largely due to the advent of container shipping which turned much of dockland into a forlorn, weed-strewn wasteland, populated only by rats and, now, yuppies.

EVEN WE CAN'T LIVE WITH THAT LOT

THE SEVENTIES AND BEYOND

When it's three o'clock in New York, it's still 1938 in London:
Bette Midler

If the sixties had ever swung, by the time the seventies came along they certainly weren't swinging any more. That nice Mr Heath (the jolly choirmaster from Broadstairs) had brought his Conservatives into power, kicking out Labour's rather dotty, rather pompous, pipe-puffing PM Harold Wilson. Heath's brief was to control the trade unions which had been squeezing the juice out of both London and the rest of the country.

By 1973, things had come to such a pass that Heath was nose to sooty nose with the miners' union, ready for the biggest show-down Britain had ever seen. Our economic situation was the worst since the war and both the Government and the unions blamed each other. In November, the now unhappy Heath called a state of emergency because he wouldn't give the miners what they demanded and they said they wouldn't dig any coal - so there! No one was allowed to heat their homes with electricity, no ads were to be lit up (no bad thing), drivers weren't allowed to go over 50 m.p.h. (unless in aeroplanes), telly had to finish at 10.30 p.m. and, worst of all, companies (from absolutely massive ones, right down to our little design studio), weren't allowed to operate for more than three days a week - which, of course, we didn't.*

Oh yes, and to cap it all, the ever-helpful IRA terrorists decided to target London to practise their bombing on.

Heath was finished. Harold Wilson and Labour bounded back for another term in which they managed to muck things up even more by giving the unions all that they'd been asking for. To the right, Heath was replaced by a handbag-swinging, permed-haired mother of twins. Margaret Thatcher became Tory leader in 1974 to everyone's surprise (except hers). James Callaghan took over the sinking government from Wilson in 1976 and seemed to dig the country into an even bigger hole. Britain was going under like the Titanic, and not even the celebrations of the Queen's twenty-five-year-reign, or the fact that we'd struck oil big-time in the North Sea could cheer things up. There were 1,500,000 on the dole, and production was as good as static.

Punk Time

Such brilliant timing. On top of all the doom and gloom, the London streets had become full of filthy, tattooed and pierced people with psychedelic spiky hair, ripped clothes, and genuinely anarchic attitudes to everything and everyone. They had nothing to give a society that had proved that it certainly didn't have anything to give them. The punks and skinheads (initially manipulated by ex-Harrow art students, Malcolm McLaren and Vivienne Westwood) symbolised what the

* It wasn't me that blacked out our windows twice a week and kept on working - honest!

new breed of Londoners thought of their elders and 'betters'. Like most anarchic movements, however, they gradually became more of a fashion statement and soon kids all over Europe were copying them in a half-baked sort of way

★ WORTH A VISIT? ★

Westwood and McLaren's seventies shop called Let it Rock, with the huge clock revolving the wrong way, is still to be visited on the kink of the King's Road, as it approaches the New King's Road. It now only sports the clothes of the hugely revered (for some bizarre reason) high-fashion designer Vivienne Westwood.

By the Way

City planners, worried about the bland 'New Yorkisation' of London's skyline, refused to allow any high buildings around that grand old lady, St Paul's. A bit late, but better than nothing.

Flood Alert

The first floods to hit London were in 1099, and since then there has been a serious flood every hundred years or so. In 1579 the Thames rose so high that there were fish left stranded on the floor of the Great Hall at Westminster, and in 1881 a tidal wave pushed the water level five metres above normal. In 1928 a sudden inrush from the North Sea burst the Thames bank in a dozen places killing fourteen people.

After the floods of 1953 an enquiry was held to see whether a barrier could be built, as they were beginning to realise that, the next time it happened, over forty-five square miles of city could be turned into a lake, not to mention the risk of a watery grave for 1,250,000 people (and what about the tubes?). Nothing much was done at the time, as they quite simply didn't know how, until scary talk of the polar icecap melting was dovetailed with the fact that London could be proved to be sinking, which doesn't seem much of a recipe for keeping your feet dry.

Apart from all this, the City was endangered from the tides that were rising by over half a metre every century.

★ WORTH A VISIT? ★

The result of all this alarmist chatter was the mighty Thames Barrier started in 1972 (not so much a dam as a machine). It is an impressive five storeys high, weighing in at 3,000 tonnes, and can rise twenty metres above the surface of the river (when turned on). So far, since its completion in 1982, it's been used nine times with complete success. There is a Visitors' Centre on the south bank at Woolwich.

Thatcher Wins

The seventies went out with the first Prime Ministress we'd ever had. The Labour Party was completely routed and the unions promptly turned about-face and did a sleazy pact with the straight-talking, no-nonsense Margaret 'She-that-must-be-obeyed' Thatcher.

THATCHER'S LONDON

The problem is that many MPs never see the London that exists beyond the wine bars and brothels of Westminster: Ken Livingstone 1987

With Margaret Thatcher in charge, London was to experience one of the most remarkable periods in its long and fascinating history. The City had survived plagues, fires, invasions and the Swingin' Sixties, but nothing could prepare her for the grocer's daughter from Grantham.

For years the gap between the rich and poor had been narrowing. The ever-expanding middle classes, realising that old houses were usually better than new, had breathed fresh life into all those central-ish areas like Clapham, Battersea and Fulham whose houses had, through neglect, become run down over the years. Thatcher's government promoted borrowing to such an extent that young couples could simply walk unannounced into any building society or bank and skip out with 100% loans, allowing them to buy bijoux flats and houses, swiftly converted, at prices that made their parents and grandparents expire. Up and up the prices went, to such an extent that at one stage anyone who actually owned anything propertywise in London could sit back and watch their bank balance blast further and further into the black on a weekly basis, without moving a muscle.

By the Way

In 1988 Mrs Grace Newbold offered £36,000 for a converted, Laura Ashley-clad shed, measuring 1.5 metres by 3.3 metres in Knightsbridge. That's how daft it had all got. The net result of this meteoric escalation in prices meant that the whole rental market began to whither. Landlords fell over each other at this once-in-a-lifetime chance to cash in their tatty and run down chips for telephone number sums.

Sleeping Rough

And what about those who didn't actually own anything, or didn't have any sort of income which allowed them to borrow? 'Tough bananas,' said the Tories! They simply watched as the others became progressively richer. Not only did renting become ludicrously expensive, but there soon became nowhere to rent, especially at the bottom end of the market. For the first time since the nineteenth century, as the unemployment figures topped 2,000,000, people who weren't winos or junkies could be seen sleeping on the streets of London in ever-increasing numbers. And did the Tories care?

In the City, young Armani-suited East End spivs (sorry – market dealers), racing their brand new Porsches and BMWs to and from their docklands penthouses, played the money markets and stock markets like monopoly. It was real weird. Everyone seemed to be doing so well, but Britain was actually producing less and less. In fact it was costing 22% more to produce 4% less. How could this be?

Black Power

In 1981, the black immigrant population, so obviously behind

this new golden door of opportunity, suddenly had enough and erupted in protest about how they were treated by police. Rioters in Brixton, South London, looted and set fire to their own premises which, in retrospect, seems a little counerproductive. The riots in Brixton sparked off a chain reaction of unrest throughout the City and its poorer suburbs. The rioters looted and set fire to their own premises which, in retrospect, seems a little counterproductive.

Never had there been such a divide between the haves and have nots. And never did Maggie care less? She was having a high old time, selling off all the public industries, like electricity and water, that had once been owned by the people, to those who had the spare cash to invest (even if they borrowed the money to do it). The unions, who'd sold out a few years earlier, realised the trap they'd fallen into far too late. They would never have the same power again.

Council Goes

As Thatcher gained more acclaim amongst the greedy middle classes, the economy looked more and more dodgy. In 1986 she joyfully scrapped the Labour-led Greater London Council that had been embarrassing her and her mates. It was a sad day for London, but not too sad. We must remember that it was the GLC that proposed the wholesale demolition of Covent Garden (which wouldn't have been a bad thing as it's turned out) and massive motorways carving their way right across the city. They were also responsible for all those acres upon dreary acres of local authority housing (especially in south London). Ken Livingstone, its popular and eccentric leader (voted runner up to the Pope in BBC Radio's 1982 'man of the year' poll) had been using the GLC unashamedly as a sledgehammer to crack Thatcherism and her government's policy on Northern Ireland.

The abolition of the GLC meant that the city would now be run by thirty-one boroughs, the City and Westminster, and sixty committees all heavily 'breathed on' by the Tories.

London was now the only major city in the West not to have its own elected government to run its affairs. Sad or what?

AND THEN . . .

It happened. The whole pile of cards tumbled on the faintest rumours from abroad. On 19th October 1988, a Monday, £50,000,000,000 was wiped off the value of shares. Forget Monopoly, the game in the City was now Snakes and Ladders – except there were no ladders. Thatcher's dream (and much of her credibility) popped like a soap bubble, and those of us who had realised it was all too good (or bad) to last, relished the spectacle of all those smart-arsed city boys falling over each other trying to off-load flash cars, luxury flats and gold-digger girl friends that they'd borrowed so much to finance.

By the Way

The price of second-hand Porsches dropped like a stone shortly after Black Monday.

. . . But

Sadly, thousands of innocent young couples were caught in the now famous 'negative equity trap', especially in London. This meant that the sum which they'd borrowed was more than the value of property they'd bought with it, which also meant that even if they could get rid of the damn thing (in a suddenly saturated property market), they'd be left with a huge debt and nowhere to live. Not only that, but the lending rate, which Thatcher had for so long made sure stayed artificially low, rocketed to new heights, so that even more people were caught with not even enough money to repay the interest, let alone the capital sum.

By the Way

Even the property market in rural France was affected by the collapse, as all those well-off Brits who'd borrowed money to buy a nice little country maison abroad, couldn't wait to get rid of them.

Parliament Revealed

With the broadcasting of Parliament on radio in April 1978 and then telly ten years later, the country was at last able to judge for itself whether Her Majesty's Government was a load of incompetent pompous prats, or a group of highly intelligent men and women, selflessly dedicated to do their best for the masses. No more need be said.

Thatcher, much to the joy of many, was finally brought to her immaculately-nyloned knees in 1990, still believing that she was invincible. She was replaced by the honest and unpretentious, but hair-tearingly boring, John Major.

LONDON SOLDIERS ON

London is a town of nice surprises and at any moment you may run into the queen doing some shopping: Michael Bateman

As old Mother London approaches her two thousandth birthday, it's worth noting that the last ten or so years have been relatively uneventful (apart from the hilarious shenanigans of the Royal Family, which I'll go into later).

Perhaps the most interesting feature of London life has been the increasing evidence of a north-south divide and a shifting of the boundary northward from the Thames to somewhere around that east-west highway that crosses from the A40 at Shepherd's Bush, over Westway, along the Euston Road and across to the City. It's reasonable to state that those who live in south London now need a very good excuse (and a passport) to venture into the north, and vice versa. In a recent survey (me and a mate and a bus pass), it was interesting to note that those in the north are even beginning to look slightly different from their southern brothers. Walk down any street in North London and you will notice, unless I'm imagining it, that the hoi-polloi generally appear more 'foreign-looking' than those south of the 'Great Divide'.

Rich Pickings

Those with money still live as close to the middle as they can afford. In the northern hemisphere the well off choose areas like Regent's Park, St John's Wood and Hampstead, while in the southern-central bit they go for Knightsbridge, Belgravia and Chelsea, not to mention the relatively-new-to-the-super-league Holland Park. Next to Holland Park, the once severely down-market Notting Hill has also witnessed an ugly-duckling-to-swan-like transformation from those crumbly squares of seedy tenements into extremely magnificent owner-occupied, *Homes and Gardens* (I nearly said *Hello*)-type homes.

By the Way

A friend of mine bought a shabby house in Notting Hill in the early fifties for £1,500. If he sold it now he'd be just short of a millionaire (or a short millionaire).

I Say, Fiona – Where Next?

The sons and daughters of the well off, particularly from the country (all rugby shirts, mobiles and those new, poncy little MG convertibles), have homed in on, and colonised, a large slice of the southern city, from Battersea through Clapham to Wandsworth. They are now threatening, believe it or not, the previously rather non-U Balham. Fortunes are still being made by ex-public school, cowboy builders and speculators who spend their lives racing around in their Toyota pickups, trying to second-guess where their hooray mates (who've now forgotten what happened to housing ten years ago) will be forced to colonise next.

★ WORTH A VISIT? ★

If you want to see them bonding *en masse* take a trip to The Ship, next to the cement works by Wandsworth Bridge.

The Ethnic Minorities

The poor old Afro-Caribbeans still seem to be holed up in the slightly less affluent, scruffier areas like Shepherd's Bush and Brixton and the huge, faceless hinterland of the deep, deep south (Lewisham, Catford, Peckham etc.).

The Asian community, who now seem to run all high street retailing, are enjoying areas like Tooting and Southall, and are making massive inroads into those dear old leafy Metroland suburbs from Ealing through to Wembley and Harrow. With their increased wealth they are now moving into staunch middle-class enclaves like the once-posh Pinner and Northwood (shock-horror).

Jewish people still tend to hang around Golders Green, Finchley and all those rather damp, depressing, north London, mock-Tudor suburbs round where the M1 begins, though the Volvo-driving, more-extreme Hasidics have moved east to places like Tottenham and Stamford Hill.

The Melting-Pot

Oddly enough, and to her great credit, unlike those of so many major cities (Beirut, Los Angeles, Paris, Belfast), London's many religions, life-styles and races seem to rub along quite well together. Okay, there's the occasional flare-up, like the aforementioned Brixton Riot caused by bad policing, or the odd punch-up at the Notting Hill Carnival, but most would admit these are few and far between, and mostly forgotten.

Royal Fun

The Royal Family should receive a lifetime award for selflessly entertaining us over the last couple of decades. In a ludicrous competition for media attention, one by one they have made complete prats of themselves (i.e. *It's a Royal Knockout**). We all coughed up for vast, lavish royal weddings, guaranteed to remind us of our lowly position, and then watched, egg on face, still metaphorically clutching our little plastic Union Jacks as the royals cavorted around the world's most luxurious playgrounds, swapping partners at will and eventually divorcing or separating at the drop of a crown. The Queen, God Save Her, seemed completely out of touch - bewildered even - and made a few dismal, 'day-in-the-life-of' documentaries to prove it. The only good thing to come out of it (apart from the laughs) was that at last the Queen, who is by far the richest woman in the world, was forced to pay tax like everyone else.

★ WORTH A VISIT? ★

In order to pay for all this and the repairs to her burnt castle at Windsor, the Queen, miserable at the end of her 'annus horribilis', decided in 1993 to open up a bit of Buckingham Palace (for August and September each year) for us all to gawp at. Reports that the Throne Room looks like a cross between a spread in *Hello* and an Indian restaurant are, I'm sure, exaggerated, but it's certainly true that only a fraction of those expected to turn up, did!

* 'It's a Knockout' *was a banal TV show where saddos from various towns competed in daft games. The junior Royals saw fit to join in, so blowing any credibility they had.*

Handy Tip: If you do decide to risk the trip, go to the loo before you visit. Despite having seventy-eight loos in the Palace, the Queen doesn't want us common folk to use any of hers. Not surprising for someone who, allegedly, takes her own lav seat wherever she goes.

Bomb Alert

Those IRA monsters, not content with wrecking their own country, decided to have a go at London, murdering our MPs and hitting the poor old girl where it hurt most. On April 24th 1993 a massive car bomb crippled the banking area (ouch!) doing over a billion pounds worth of damage. Eventually a cordon was thrown round the 'square mile' in June of the same year, manned by policemen on the look out for anyone with a dodgy looking motor – or a Northern Irish accent.

Then, after nearly two decades of derisive, divisive Tory rule, a strangely united but severely constipated country gave one final shove and removed the blockage, giving the boyish Tony Blair and his New Labour Party an embarrassingly easy passage to victory in 1997. The country and particularly London (where they all lived) gave a huge sigh of relief. New Labour's start has been, to say the least, shaky, but as this little book wings its way to the printers, it looks like London will once again have its own council and mayor (maybe even Ken Livingstone), and, with a bit of luck, at last will be able to make decisions for itself again.

AND NOW?

London is a university with 10 million graduates qualified to live and let live: Oliver St. John Gogarty 1937

So what are we left with after such a phenomenal history? Why do people, like me, still live here? Well, it certainly isn't the prettiest city in the world (unless you're reading this on Waterloo Bridge at sunset) and, to be honest, it certainly isn't the cleanest or tidiest (unless you hang around IKEA a lot). The Underground has got to be one of the most expensive and inefficient in the world, and trying to get anywhere on the surface is virtually impossible. Even when you do manage to get your car into the centre there's nowhere to park and, if we believe the statistics, nowhere to breathe. Oh, yes, and London is one of the most pricey cities you can find, with citizens whose lower-than-average income (Europe-wise) certainly can't match up to it. Worse still, despite its reputation as a happening place, it still boasts licensing laws that are like an admonishing finger waving at anyone who doesn't gulp down their last drink by 11 o'clock (when most foreign cities are waking up).

Summing up, London is like the worst and the best girlfriend I ever had. On the one hand she's cruel, slightly grubby, often violent, always expensive, occasionally unfriendly and terribly unforgiving (actually she sounds a lot better than the worst girlfriend I ever had).

But . . .

On the other, to continue the female analogy, she is the most grown up, subtly sexy, always exciting, wonderfully unpredictable, unashamedly 'sorted' lady in the world. She never feels the need to look over her shoulder to see what others are doing and never bothers to boast or apologise for all the crazy and much copied things that have been born out of her teeming streets. But, most of all, anyone who's ever lived here for any length of time must agree that the very, very bestest thing about London is that, far more than any other city that I've ever been to, she is happy to let those who live within her boundaries - whoever they may be - be whatever they want to be whenever they want to be it (and that's one hell of a lot of bees).

This book has been my rather weedy tribute to my home town and all those who have, in her long and lurid history, made her what she is and hopefully always will be - in the words of Tina Turner - simply the best!

BIBLIOGRAPHY

I recommend the following for further reading:

* *Crime and Scandal - the Black Plaque Guide to London*, Felix Barker & Denise Silvester-Carr (Constable)

* *A Medieval History of the Kings and Queens of England*, Cliford Brewer (Published by the author)

* *The Clink Prison*, E.J.Burford, (The Clink Prison)

* *The Shell Guide to the History of London*, WR Dalzell (Michael Joseph)

* *Crime and Society in England 1750-1900*, Clive Elmsley, (Longman)

* *Punishment and Torture*, Karen Farrington, (Hamlyn)

* *The London Nobody Knows*, Geoffrey Fletcher (Penguin)

* *Encyclopaedia of Britain*, Bamber Gasgoine, (Macmillan)

* *Chronicle of Britain*, Edited by Henrietta Heald, (Jacques Legrand)

* *A History of London*, Alan Ivimey, Sampson Low, (Marston & Co)

* *London (Eyewitness Travel Guides)*, Michael Leapman, (Dorling Kindersley)

* *Oxford Illustrated History of Britain*, Kenneth O. Morgan (editor), (OUP)

* *London - a Social History*, Roy Porter, (Hamish Hamilton)

* *Book of Strange Stories, Amazing Facts*, (Readers Digest)

* *London and Its People*, John Richardson, (Barrie and Jenkins)

* *The Story of Britain: A People's History*, Roy Strong, (Pimlico)

* *A Traveller's History of London*, Richard Tames, (The Windrush Press)

* *The London Encyclopaedia*, B. Weinrob & C. Hibbert (editors), (Macmillan)

* *London*, Henry B Wheatley, (J.M.Dent)

* *English Costume*, Doreen Yarwood, (B.T.Batsford Ltd)

* Plus the magnificent London Section of the Guildhall Library

LONDON'S KINGS AND QUEENS

HOUSES OF CERDIC AND DENMARK
927-939   ATHELSTAN
939-946   EDMUND I
946-955   EADRED
955-959   EADWIG
959-975   EDGAR I
975-978   EDWARD I (The Martyr)
978-1016   ETHELRED (The Unready)
1016   EDMUND II (Ironside)
1016-1035   CNUTE
1035-1040   HAROLD I
1040-1042   HARDACNUTE
1042-1066   EDWARD II (The Confessor)
1066   HAROLD II

THE HOUSE OF NORMANDY
1066-1087   WILLIAM I (The Conqueror)
1087-1100   WILLIAM II (Rufus)
1100-1135   HENRY I
1135-1154   STEPHEN

THE HOUSE OF PLANTAGENETS
1154-1189   HENRY II
1189-1199   RICHARD I (Coeur de Lion)
1199-1216   JOHN (Lackland)
1216-1272   HENRY III
1272-1307   EDWARD I (Longshanks)
1307-1327   EDWARD II
1327-1377   EDWARD III
1377-1399   RICHARD II

THE HOUSE OF LANCASTER
1399-1413   HENRY IV
1413-1422   HENRY V
1422-1471   HENRY VI

THE HOUSE OF YORK
1461–1483	EDWARD IV
1483	EDWARD V
1483–1485	RICHARD III

THE HOUSE OF TUDOR
1485–1509	HENRY VII
1509–1547	HENRY VIII
1547–1553	EDWARD VI
1553	LADY JANE GREY
1553–1558	MARY I (Mary Tudor)
1558–1603	ELIZABETH I

THE HOUSE OF STUART
1603–1625	JAMES I
1625–1649	CHARLES I
1649–1660	COMMONWEALTH
1660–1685	CHARLES II
1685–1688	JAMES II
1689–1702	WILLIAM
and	
1689–1694	MARY II
1702–1714	ANNE

THE HOUSE OF HANOVER
1714–1727	GEORGE I
1727–1760	GEORGE II
1760–1820	GEORGE III
1811–1820	REGENCY
1820–1830	GEORGE IV
1830–1837	WILLIAM IV
1837–1901	VICTORIA

THE HOUSE OF SAXE-COBURG AND GOTHA
1901–1910	EDWARD VII
1910–1936	GEORGE V
1936	EDWARD VIII
1936–1952	GEORGE VI
1952–	ELIZABETH II

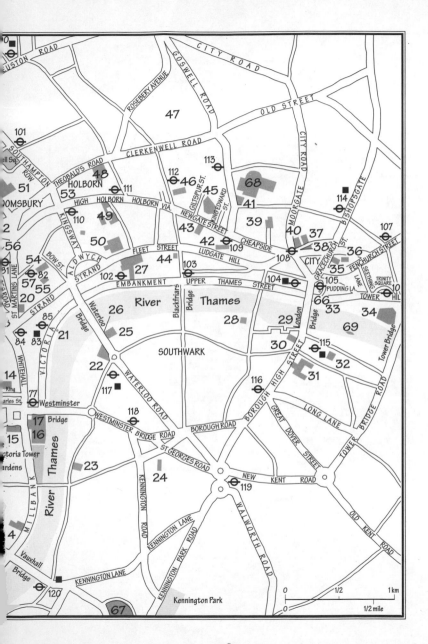

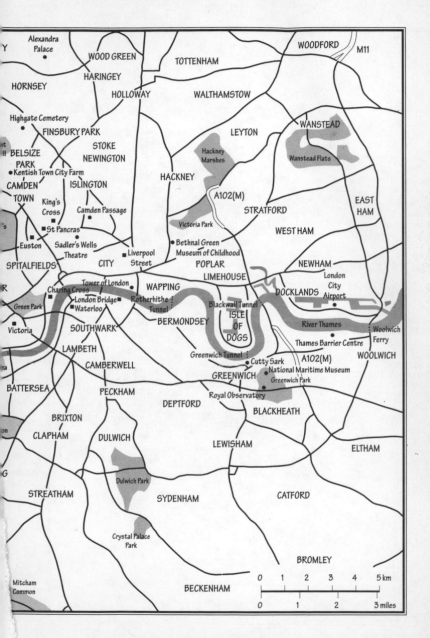

CENTRAL LONDON

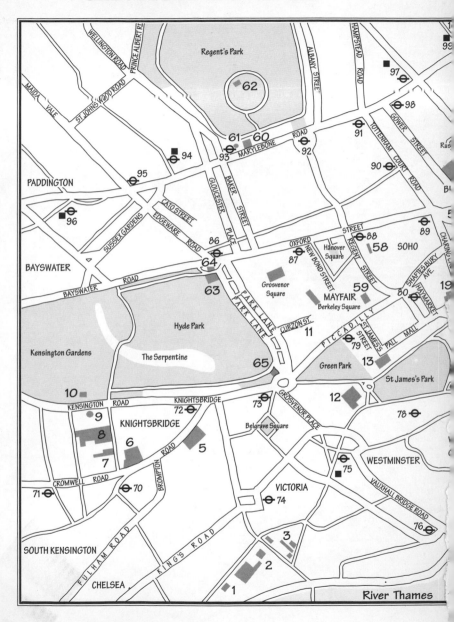

Regent's Park

62

WELLINGTON ROAD

PRINCE ALBERT RD

ST JOHN'S WOOD RD

ALBANY STREET

HAMPSTEAD ROAD

GOWER STREET

99

97

98

91

TOTTENHAM COURT ROAD

90

Rus

MAIDA VALE

61 60

93 MARYLEBONE ROAD

92

94

95

PADDINGTON

96

CATO STREET

EDGEWARE ROAD

GLOUCESTER PLACE

BAKER STREET

86

64

STREET

88

89

CHARING CRS

OXFORD

87 NEW BOND STREET

Hanover Square

58 SOHO

REGENT STREET

SHAFTESBURY AVE.

BAYSWATER

SUSSEX GARDENS

BAYSWATER ROAD

63

Grosvenor Square

MAYFAIR 59

80 19

HAYMARKET

Hyde Park

PARK LANE

Berkeley Square

Kensington Gardens

The Serpentine

65

CURZON ST.

11

PICCADILLY

ST JAMES'S STREET

79

PALL MALL

13

Green Park

St James's Park

10

KENSINGTON ROAD

KNIGHTSBRIDGE

72

73

GROSVENOR PLACE

12

78

9

KNIGHTSBRIDGE

Belgrave Square

8

6

BROMPTON ROAD

5

WESTMINSTER

7

75

CROMWELL ROAD

70

VAUXHALL BRIDGE ROAD

71

VICTORIA

74

76

3

KING'S ROAD

FULHAM ROAD

2

SOUTH KENSINGTON

1

CHELSEA

River Thames

OUTER LONDON

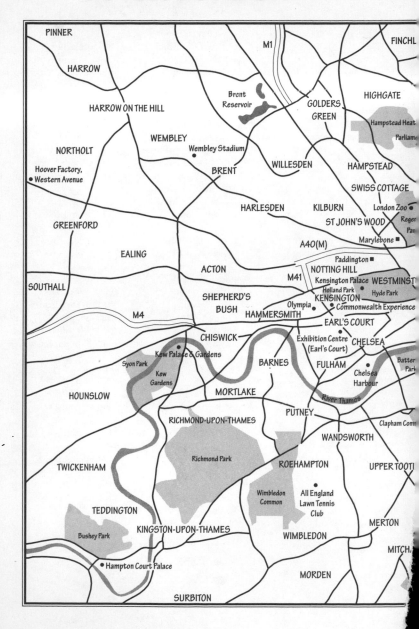

KEY

BUILDINGS AND MUSEUMS

1 National Army Museum
2 Royal Hospital
3 Chelsea Barracks
4 Tate Gallery
5 Harrods
6 Victoria & Albert Museum
7 Science Museum
8 Imperial College
9 Royal Albert Hall
10 Albert Memorial
11 Shepherd's Market
12 Buckingham Palace
13 St James's Palace
14 Cabinet War Offices
15 Westminster Abbey
16 Houses of Parliament
17 Big Ben
18 Trafalgar Square
19 National Gallery
20 St Martin-in-the-Fields
21 Cleopatra's Needle
22 Royal Festival Hall
23 Lambeth Palace
24 Imperial War Museum
25 Royal National Theatre
26 Museum of Moving Image
27 Inns of Court
28 Globe Theatre
29 The Clink
30 Southwark Cathedral
31 Guy's Hospital
32 London Dungeon
33 Billingsgate
34 Tower of London
35 Leadenhall Market
36 Lloyds
37 Stock Exchange
38 The Royal Exchange
39 Guildhall
40 Bank of England
41 Museum of London
42 St Paul's Cathedral
43 Old Bailey
44 St Bride's Church
45 St Bart's Hospital
46 Smithfields Market
47 House of Detention
48 Gray's Inn
49 Lincoln's Inn
50 Royal Courts of Justice
51 British Museum
52 Centre Point
53 St Etheldreda's Church
54 Royal Opera House
55 London Transport Museum
56 Leicester Square
57 Covent Garden
58 Carnaby Street
59 Royal Academy
60 Madam Tussaud's
61 Planetarium
62 Open Air Theatre
63 Speaker's Corner
64 Marble Arch
65 Apsley House
66 Monument
67 The Oval
68 The Barbican
69 HMS Belfast

MAINLINE AND UNDERGROUND STATIONS

70 South Kensington
71 Gloucester Road
72 Knightsbridge
73 Hyde Park Corner
74 Sloane Square
75 Victoria
76 Pimlico
77 Westminster
78 St James's Park
79 Green Park
80 Piccadilly
81 Leicester Square
82 Covent Garden
83 Charing Cross Mainline
84 Charing Cross
85 Embankment
86 Marble Arch
87 Bond Street
88 Oxford Circus
89 Tottenham Court Road
90 Goodge Street
91 Warren Street
92 Regent's Park
93 Baker Street
94 Marylebone
95 Edgware Road
96 Paddington
97 Euston
98 Euston Square
99 St Pancras
100 Kings Cross
101 Russell Square
102 Temple
103 Blackfriars
104 Cannon Street
105 Monument
106 Tower Hill
107 Aldgate
108 Bank
109 St Paul's
110 Holborn
111 Chancery Lane
112 Farringdon
113 Barbican
114 Liverpool Street
115 London Bridge
116 Borough
117 Waterloo
118 Lambeth North
119 Elephant & Castle
120 Vauxhall

■ *Mainline station*
⊖ *Underground station*